## Praise for *Slug an*

"Megan Milks is the most interest There! I said it. Milks smashes fiction and genre together. Milks destroys boredom! Milks stans fanfic, retells the New Narrative, lights a million candles at the altar of queer and trans experimental literature, sends love letters to Kathy Acker and Samuel R. Delany and Ovid, hate-reads Sweet Valley High in the sexiest and most disturbing ways. You will never look at Tegan and Sara—or slugs, or tomatoes—in the same way again. Be careful: this collection will permanently change the way you read. Don't say I didn't warn you."

**—ANDREA LAWLOR**, author of
*Paul Takes the Form of a Mortal Girl*

"*Slug and Other Stories* mixes pop culture, Greek myth, queer feminism, and childhood nostalgia into a gory and gorgeous mess. I got my hands dirty digging into Megan Milks's sanguine collection of short stories. This prose oozes. This prose dripped perversely into my consciousness and stuck. Only a steady and sagacious writer like Milks can make paddling through this kind of muck so absolutely pleasurable."

**—AMBER DAWN**, author of *Sub Rosa*

"Video-game logic, middle school best-friend clubs, choose your own adventure: Megan Milks both critiques and indulges in pop-culture forms, often by way of viscid zoological/extraterrestrial avatars, and does so while saying profound things about trans bodies, intimacy, and vulnerability. How did they do all this? They are so cool, and I definitely want to be their friend."

**—JEANNE THORNTON**, author of *Summer Fun*

"Few writers are able to surprise and thrill me like Megan Milks does. *Slug and Other Stories* moves from fantasy to embodiment, inventing an eroticism that explodes binaries in ways that are both destabilizing and a real turn on."

**—DODIE BELLAMY**, author of
*When the Sick Rule the World*

"These stories are pure force: they norm deviance, make violence effulgent, ungender and regender sexualities. Each story is a kitsch throwback to when reading was a fun choose your own adventure. These stories are not just carnal, not just animalistic, not just girly: they're amphibian, our full corporeal tenderized to satisfaction, which is to say—hot."

**—LILY HOANG, author of _A Bestiary_**

"Genre conventions are commonly thought of as restrictive rules, but in these stories Megan Milks shows that these conventions can be agents of perversion, both glaringly porous and ridiculously invasive. Over the course of the book, Milks invokes and employs the genre conventions of fan fiction on, for example, Kafka's _Metamorphosis_ and teen comedies, then mixes in young adult novels, video games, choose-your-own adventure tales, epistolary novels, gothic tales, family romances, and 'Trauma-rama' entries, until this melee of genres interrupt each other, parasite each other, distort each other. The result of this romp is absurd, grotesque, parapornographic, violent, gurlesque, but most of all hilarious in a deadpan kind of way."

**—JOHANNES GÖRANSSON,**
**author of _Haute Surveillance_**

"Wittig's _The Lesbian Body_ goes superfreak in this celebration of excess, this inquiry into boundarylessness, this exercise in genre-fuck, this slug-and/or-be-slugged fest. In a collection whose voices range from hard-boiled to hyperbolic to hysterical, Milks seriously probes the implications of social constructionism: we've made a monster (albeit sometimes hot, albeit sometimes queer) of the sexed body, individual and politic. Somehow, happily, Milks keep it comic too. Lots of parts and effluvia, no gratuitous grossness!"

**—ALEXANDRA CHASIN, author of _Brief_**

"Megan Milks's collection is a fearless romp through the post-avant wasteland of fictions both Lynchian and Homeric. Milks puts Shelley Jackson's _The Melancholy of Anatomy_ through a cement mixer, grinding out tales as sure to delight as they radically defamiliarize. Here, Sweet Valley Twins gets a reboot finally worthy of the world their YA books helped to make weird. Milks is a master of the absurd grotesque, and _Slug and Other Stories_ is their powerful annunciation."

**—DAVIS SCHNEIDERMAN, author of _Multifesto_**

# SLUG

### AND OTHER STORIES

# MEGAN MILKS

**THE FEMINIST PRESS**
AT THE CITY UNIVERSITY OF NEW YORK
NEW YORK CITY

Published in 2021 by the Feminist Press
at the City University of New York
The Graduate Center
365 Fifth Avenue, Suite 5406
New York, NY 10016

feministpress.org

First Feminist Press edition 2021

This story collection was originally published in different form as *Kill Marguerite and Other Stories* by Emergency Press in 2014. The book has since been revised and expanded. See page 247 for further publication details.

This book was made possible thanks to a grant from New York State Council on the Arts with the support of Governor Andrew M. Cuomo and the New York State Legislature.

Second printing July 2023

Cover design by Xander Marro
Text design by Drew Stevens

**Library of Congress Cataloging-in-Publication Data**
Names: Milks, Megan, author.
Title: Slug : and other stories / Megan Milks.
Description: First Feminist Press edition. | New York City : Feminist
    Press, 2021.
Identifiers: LCCN 2021029487 (print) | LCCN 2021029488 (ebook) | ISBN
    9781952177842 (paperback) | ISBN 9781952177859 (ebook)
Subjects: LCGFT: Experimental fiction. | Short stories.
Classification: LCC PS3613.I532274 S58 2021 (print) | LCC PS3613.I532274
    (ebook) | DDC 813/.6--dc23
LC record available at https://lccn.loc.gov/2021029487
LC ebook record available at https://lccn.loc.gov/2021029488

PRINTED IN THE UNITED STATES OF AMERICA

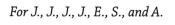

*For J., J., J., J., E., S., and A.*

"A kind of liquid jelly is dripping all over me."

—DODIE BELLAMY, *Cunt-Ups*

# CONTENTS

*SLUG*

Patty will ask her date to walk her to the door. Patty will play I'm Frightened and Scared to Be Alone in the Deep Dark Night. Of course he will accompany her, despite the drizzle. He will be happy to. Delighted. Then Patty will push him up against the door so that he's straddling the doorknob, so it's pressing into his ass crack, and shove his shoulders back, hard, and suck his tongue, hard, and rub his crotch, hard, and push his arms up and over his head and hold them there so that he is her prisoner. It is a good thing she wore her bitch boots tonight. It is a good thing she dressed prepared. She will take out her pocketknife and flip up the knife part and she will tickle him with the blade, slowly, deliberately, and she will increase pressure as she moves the knife down from his sternum to his pelvis. His stomach will retract involuntarily.

She will unlock the door, swing it wide, and step back, return to I'm Frightened and squeak, It Looks Like There Could Be a Burglar. Won't You Please Check? I'm So Scared. He will play along, say, It Would Be My Pleasure to Check for the Burglar. Stay behind Me. Stay Close. And he will grab her wrist firmly and push her behind him, stroking her wrist suggestively. It will be nice.

Patty's date works hard to clear his throat. The first try miserably fails. He tries again, succeeds, changes the car radio to smooth jazz. Patty uncrosses, then recrosses her legs, begins to clench and unclench her thighs under her plain black skirt.

Patty is a wicked schoolgirl with an S-M fetish. Underneath her plain black skirt is a honking big strap-on. (She makes a note to self: purchase harness and dildo, a formidable dildo.) At her command, he will get on his hands and knees and enjoy the rug burn, you pathetic motherfucker. Patty is a vicious cunt in bondage gear, with a whip and not afraid to use it, worm. Patty likes to be tied up, chained up with needles through her nipples, getting burned to blood-black with cigarettes and branding irons. Patty enjoys biting and being bitten, hard, like starved vampires. She also enjoys bestiality; triple, quadruple penetration; and feverish, drugged-up sex parties. Sex parties have lots of drugs. What kinds of drugs will Patty's sex party have? Patty is in the middle of being consensually gangbanged, which means violence and overwhelming numbers of cocks at once. Patty is the one with the cock, and she is making him eat it, swallow it, gag.

"You're not giving me much to go on," he says.

He has been talking all this time.

She will smear his forehead with menstrual blood, then slice a line in his lower abdomen and rub her face in his blood and guts. And shit. Shit will be smeared everywhere. She will hang him upside down, ankles chained together and thighs caked with shit. She will leave him there with her formidable dildo in his asshole and slashes in his heels so he cannot walk when she unties him. She will be ruthless and loyal. After she slashes his heels, she will check in with a Baby,

Are You Okay? Tell Me You're Okay, and take out his gag so he can say so. Then she will shove the gag back down his throat, kneel before him, and masturbate where he can see her, inches from his nose and mouth.

Patty shrugs, smiles lazily over at him, lost in her dreaming.

His tongue in her mouth is slithery and warm, then a lifeless slab of muscle to her weak response. Fumbling and finally dead. Retracted. Suck.

Patty clenches and unclenches her thighs, faster, faster, until she is done.

When she is done, she thanks him, they should do it again sometime.

Then she slams the car door and hurries through the rain to her apartment building, stepping on a slug that's sprawled out to suck in the moisture. Ugh. That squishes. She scrapes the slug guts off on the doorstep and lets herself inside.

IN THE KITCHEN, Patty grabs a used glass and fills it with filtered water. Gulps it down. Stands there with her fingers on her lips, thinking he wasn't so bad. She could have been nicer. She could have tried harder. Made something happen. But what had he looked like? She remembers the nervous gurgling in particular. The meek way he cleared his throat. The tapping on the steering wheel, anxious, impatient.

She had made him impatient. That's funny. She had had an effect. He probably would've been too safe in bed, anyway. He would've wanted her to act like a girl.

Everyone is always too safe. Probably. What do normal people do?

They take off their shoes and makeup and go to bed.

Patty takes off her shoes and makeup and goes to bed.

Patty has not closed her window, despite the drizzle, which has now turned to rain. There is a lot of rain. It is raining hard. The rain is hard. Hard rain. Getting harder. The rain is getting harder and harder until it is too hard for anyone to handle.

Patty, close the window! Patty, close the window! But Patty does not close the window.

ONCE, A LONG while ago, Patty was in love with a man she met online. He had responded to an ad, or she had responded to his, and they had had a feverish exchange in which each had confessed her or his own and encouraged one another's perversities. He wrote every morning; she responded dutifully before retiring for the night. In their emails, they would each describe her or his every desire in obsessive detail, carefully crafting fetish after fetish with the intent to elicit the most violent desire and intrigue from her or his reader. For Patty, masturbation had never been so good.

After a time, they began to write erotic stories for each other. Patty wrote rottingdonquix a story after *Story of O*, in which O grew a cock and turned the tables on her Master, reducing him to the most obsequious and pathetic of slaves. Rottingdonquix responded with a story inspired, she found out later, by Sacher-Masoch, in which his Venus was not so much wearing furs as she was covered in fur, for she was a vampiric werewolf who feverishly desired to suck the blood from the narrator's cock. Patty had written him another story, in which Bataille's bull's-eye was passed back and forth from orifice to orifice until finally, in the midst of passionate intercourse, it burst in the protagonist's throbbing cunt. He wrote back with an overwrought masturbation fantasy revolving around an onyx engagement ring. Upon reading it, she experienced the strong stench of rotten eggs and could not bring herself to reply.

Weeks passed.

One day, missing the thrill of rottingdonquix's emails, Patty wrote him with the suggestion that they meet in person. He agreed.

He was bloated and ugly. She left with a sneer on her face.

That was the end of love.

PATTY IS IN her bed masturbating. She has tied her date up with fishing line that cuts into his skin, leaves blood blisters pooling subcutaneously. She does the same with his cock, which is always fully erect, then kneels in front of him, makes eye contact, and extracts her tongue slowly, torturously, until the tip just touches the head of it. He moans behind his gag. Saliva gets stuck in his throat and he tries to clear it, takes two tries, three, is perpetually clearing his throat. Patty's tongue has not moved from its tentative perch on the tip of his cock. Then she lurches forward to wrap it around the head while grabbing the ends of the fishing line with her hand and tugging, gently, gently, until he comes. He comes five more times as she frees his cock from the fishing line.

Patty does not come, because Patty's fantasy is dumb. Mindless S-M drivel. Patty can do better.

She tries again.

Patty is masturbating. Patty grows a cock and it extends, fully engorged and throbbing with sensation. Patty's cock extends and extends, quivering in the air it is exposed in, then slowly curves backward and into her cunt. Patty's cock tentatively probes her cunt before beginning to fuck it, first leisurely, then hard, pummeling it in sync with the hard rain outside.

Patty's cock and Patty's cunt come at the same time.

Patty comes.

Patty drifts off.

Patty still has not closed the window.

TAP, TAP. TAP.

Slug hangs down from the top of the window, suctioning his wet body, his enormous foot, to the exterior pane. There is a loud and sustained squerk as Slug navigates the window-pane at his infuriatingly slow pace.

Patty stirs from her half sleep.

Two sets of tentacles probe the glass.

Tap, tap.

Tap.

The incoming air is cold and moist. Patty stirs again, shivers. Her nipples tighten.

Slug's tentacles fidget impatiently as they work to gauge the size of the opening. The window is not wide enough for Slug's impressive girth, but Slug is both lubricated and stretchy. He begins the process of entering her room.

Patty blinks.

Slug is six feet of pure muscle struggling to get through her window. Slug is a rippling lump of skin shimmering with beads of rain on top of a more general wetness. Slug is multicolored, translucent skinned, eyeless, faceless, hairless. Slug's intricate underbelly is lined with undulating muscles that tremble against the pane, excreting stickiness, excreting slime.

Patty, torn between horror and desire, cannot bring herself to look away.

By now Slug has pushed a quarter of his body through the window, attaching himself to the other side of the glass.

He pulls himself farther forward, inch by thick inch, up the glass until his full length is inside. A pause, a shudder of slick skin, before he continues. He crawls along the wall, staining it with his wet trail as he nears her bed. Hanging down, he fills her nostrils with the smell of fresh soil. His tentacles toy with her hair.

Slug curves toward her, his back end vertical, attached to the wall, his front end suctioning itself to her shoulder, kneading her skin with his underbelly: like an introduction, like saying hello.

Patty sucks in her breath.

*Hello.*

He twists toward her head. Soon there is mucus creeping through her hair. His front end gropes her forehead, sticky lubricant oozing into her brows, clumping her eyelashes together, choking her nasal passage with a swamp musk. She opens her mouth to breathe. He enters, gropes around, sucks on her tongue noisily with the front portion of his foot, and pushes forward until her throat closes up and rejects him. He pulls himself out with reluctance, works his way to her torso. Past her chin, along her neck, he slurps noisily, slowly, taking his time. The bedsprings bark. As he moves forward, he shoves her camisole down, the thin straps breaking, and flattens both breasts with his weight, his belly gripping and releasing her nipples rhythmically. She finds herself making soft gurgling sounds deep in her larynx. Slug gurgles Slug's reply.

Then he slugs himself down, less leisurely now, hugging the curves of her abdomen, his tentacles seeking her tunnel. Slowed by an unruly nest of hairs, his lubricant smooths the way, and—at last—he probes her slit, first tentative, then with force. He inches forward, nudging her thighs apart.

Patty's hands claw at the sheets. The wind rustles trees outside. The wind enters the room triumphantly, amplifying the scent of swamp that is beginning to suffocate Patty. Slug surges forward, stretching himself taut, easily eight feet long, digging, digging as deep as he can, the bed creaking with every insatiable thrust. Lodged inside her vulva, his front half shifts to suit her, curving back and downward. The rest of his body, resting on her torso, kneads her flesh raw. Under his weight, she struggles to further open her thighs. It is difficult—he is massive, his skin so slippery—but she needs to show him: more, please, more. She wants all of him. Slug manages to pull a few more inches of his body inside, his trembling underbelly attacking her canal from all angles, speeding its tempo to frantic bursts. Faster. Harder. Her muscles tense. Faster. Harder. Almost. Slug gently chews at her cervix, bringing her to excessive climax. Patty arches, kicks, sucks in so deep she nearly swallows her tongue.

The room is heavy with dampness. Slug slows to a hum. Then he extracts himself slowly, the suction stubborn, painful to break, and rests on top of her, his underbelly engulfing her body in its folds.

Slug has crushed Patty. Patty has died.

SLUG KISSES PATTY. Slug kisses Patty until Patty can't breathe. Slug is in her nostrils and in her mouth. Slug's mucus drips down her throat and fills her lungs. Slug's mucus fills her body.

Patty is drenched in Slug. Her eyes are slimed shut, her hair slimed into new skin. Her face is slimed into an amorphous blob. Patty tries to move, but Slug's weight prevents her. She chokes a little, learning how to breathe again.

His work done, Slug releases her and crawls onto the wall

behind her. He creeps back over to the window and perches, his head turned toward her, his tentacles dancing. He emits a gurgle. It seems to mean Come with Me.

Though she cannot see the limbs that are no longer there, Patty understands that her body has changed. She rolls onto her belly, finding that she can feel where she is with two sets of tentacles attached to what used to be her face. She tries to talk but can only gurgle back.

Slug nods: he understands.

Patty follows Slug through the trees behind her building, their slime smoothing them over wet leaves and limp twigs, over thin gravel, the occasional rotting pine cone, until they come to a heavy dampness under a half-fallen tree trunk. Slug turns back and nudges her playfully, his tentacles fondling hers. Then he leads her up the trunk and out onto one of its outstretched limbs. There they mate, Slug showing her how to wrap around his length as he wraps around hers, so that they are a DNA strand, a corkscrew, hanging down from the limb on one rope of slime. It is easy, this full-body writhing. For a long while they are content to lick each other, lapping up one another's slime and producing more in its place.

This is the wettest Patty has ever been. Her body is in full tremble, every pore of her skin secreting slime, every nerve channeling excitement.

Suddenly she feels a new sensation: her cock is beginning to protrude translucent from her mantle to wrap around Slug's protruding cock, its sensitivity heightened with every fondle of the wind. Like their bodies, their cocks writhe around each other until they are intertwined. Then their cocks begin to expand, throbbing and massive, together forming an intricate flower that dangles down from their hanging bodies.

Patty and Slug tighten their embrace further and further still, in sync with their pulsating cocks. Tighter, tighter, tighter; their cocks throb, begging for release. Finally they ejaculate, each fertilizing the other in an extended, exorbitant climax that ends all time and thought.

Patty is dizzy. Patty is exhausted. Patty has more work to do.

Because Slug's cock is stuck in Patty's cock, Patty must begin to chew it away, being careful not to chew off her own cock in the process. As Patty gently chews, Slug writhes around her body and gurgles in pleasure, in pain. When she is done, Slug drops down and sprawls on the leaf-matted forest ground for a moment, recovering. Then he creeps away.

Now Patty is alone, dangling precariously from the tree limb. She tries swinging herself over to the trunk but, fatigued, cannot build momentum. Like her lover, she allows herself to fall from the rope of slime to the soft ground. Though the fall is not long, the impact stings.

Here Patty rests. What will Patty do next?

# THE STRANDS

Tegan's pillow was growing hair. Not the pillow she slept on, but its twin, the one she faced at night. She woke with her fingers wound tight through the tangle.

Tegan extricated her hand and sat up. She was alone in bed, as she had been for months—except for Jack at the foot and this nest at the head. It was a strangeness. In a loose spiral, it rose from the pillowcase. Not straight up—it twisted toward Tegan. It sought.

Plegh. A strand had squirmed past her lips. She extracted it. Long and dark and jangling. Familiar. Whose hair *was* this? It certainly wasn't Tegan's—short and straight and wispy. Stop pretending. Tegan knew. Of course Tegan knew. It was Sarah's.

Nearly a year after their breakup, Sarah was still shedding. Still sprawling. Still there.

Tegan glared upward, at no one. Are you casting spells on me? she demanded of the ceiling. She waited for an answer. None came.

There are layers to any strand. The outermost layer is constructed of dead cells. The next layer is made up of keratin (dead), which determines the strand's strength, elasticity, color, and shape. Inside that is the medulla (also dead), which is packed loosely, sloppily, disorganized. Only the thickest hairs have it.

Sarah's hair was thick. Voluminous. Unruly. It collected in corners, loose balls that gathered dust. Tegan had grown accustomed to finding it clinging to the feet of her socks, threaded into the knit of her sweaters. Strands floated out from the back of Sarah's chair. They wrapped around drains, catching grime. Once, Tegan suggested Sarah cut it. Sarah laughed.

After she left, Tegan swept up the hair of ten heads. She would have liked to call it all Sarah's but Tegan had hair too. And there was Jack, the cat. Very hairy.

Ha ha.

Ha—

Tegan had met Sarah last summer, outside a bar where Tegan was playing volleyball on a women's rec league, her contributions restrained and half-hearted. Stuck in a too-tight, too-sweaty binder, she couldn't commit to the ball or her team or the whole sporty scene. New to this town, she knew she ought to meet people, but none of this—the flip-flops, the mosquitoes, the pale, spitty beer—was very Tegan. Tegan would have rather been indoors alone, watching the new *Mildred Pierce*.

Sarah was at the bar with a friend, unaware of volleyball until four brawny women in tank tops filed in for the bathroom, tracking sand. Sarah and friend went out to join the sidelines for the novelty and the ogling. Sarah's friend Jen was friends with Tegan's friend Jenn. Tegan and Sarah looked each other up and down, pretending not to be looking. I'm Tegan, Tegan said. I'm Sarah. With an *h*.

Like popular musical duo Tegan and Sara Quin, this Tegan and this Sarah were lesbians. They knew this because they were both at women's volleyball though neither of them felt it was very *them*, and because, like Tegan and Sara, Tegan and Sarah had good haircuts. Unlike celebrity Sara's haircut, Sarah's haircut was, above the undercut, full and free and wild, bursting from its topknot. Unlike celebrity Tegan's haircut, Tegan's haircut was clipped on the sides and fuller on top, a definitively butch style.

Unlike celebrity Sara, Sarah was definitively femme, which Tegan knew because across the chest of her pale-pink tee sprawled the words "lazy femme." Unlike celebrity Tegan, this Tegan appeared definitively butch, though Tegan fretted over the fit. *Am* I butch? she asked pointedly whenever she was called that. No one knew the right answer.

Unlike celebrity Tegan and unlike this Sarah, this Tegan maybe was trans, though she had been trying hard not to be, didn't want to be, yet. Tegan wanted to stay Tegan. But who was Tegan? That was the problem. In this new scene she was blurry around the edges, unknown and so far unknowable.

When she met Sarah, she felt more solidly herself than she had felt in years. Do you know about the subgenre of Tegan and Sara fan fiction called "quincest"? Tegan asked. Sarah raised a provocative eyebrow and leaned forward. Does it involve Tegan and Sarah . . . fucking? The way she said "Sarah" made it clear who she meant, and the way she said "fucking," what.

And they became, like Tegan and Sara, twins.

Sarah, like Sara, was sweeter looking and prettier than Tegan. Tegan, like Tegan, had the better tattoos.

> It is important to understand the hair growth cycle in order to recognize and understand many of the problems you can encounter with your hair. Hair growth is a complex and cyclically controlled process with three basic stages. The first stage is the active growth stage (anagen), which may last for two to seven years. In this stage, the hair follicle grows deeper within the scalp until a bulb forms at the bottom. The bulb becomes attached to a web of connective structures that support the growth of the hair shaft.

Tegan adopted a power stance and aimed her power at the pillow. She leaned forward and grabbed the hair nest. I'm not afraid of you, she muttered. The nest stayed stuck. It wasn't loose, Tegan realized, but lodged inside the pillow's fibers, rooted by some hardy hair heart.

Tegan sighed. With Sarah, things always stayed stuck.

Poor Tegan. This relationship had never been good for her. Them. Good for them. Tegan was still getting used to their new pronouns, had to rewrite them in their head.

Tegan carried the pillow outside; it sagged between their arms. Into the trash bin it went. They considered burning the pillow but didn't want to give Sarah that drama. No fire for Sarah. The garbage would have to be enough. Tegan let the lid clang down and went back inside to wash their hands.

In the bathroom mirror, Tegan searched for changes the way they searched every day. The sharp new hair pushing out from their upper lip was strange and exciting. Tegan traced it anxiously, trying to find its boundaries. No sideburns yet. Meanwhile their fade had faded; their forelock had drooped. Tegan needed a haircut.

> First used only in reference to plants [. . .] *grow* spreads out to mean numerous things: from "of a plant to manifest vigorous life" to "of living bodies: to increase gradually in size by natural development"; "[. . .] to increase gradually in magnitude, quantity, or degree"; and "of the sea: to swell." Which is to say, growth is a matter of extension, vigor, and volume as well as verticality.[1]

On the phone to make a hair appointment, Tegan realized what day it was. Twins Day. National Twins Day. Marked in bright black in their slim weekly planner.

Tegan and Sarah had long-standing plans to attend this year's Twins Day Festival. It had been Tegan's idea, a joke, really, that Sarah took seriously, made serious, made hers. Tegan smiled along, unconvinced, having already done

---

1. Kathryn Bond Stockton, *The Queer Child, or Growing Sideways in the Twentieth Century* (Durham, NC: Duke University Press, 2009), 11.

the research, knowing the events were for real twins, not make-believe lesbian twinsies like Sarah and Tegan. You have to show your birth certificates, Tegan had cautioned. We can be creative, said Sarah. Maybe we should respect the twins community, Tegan suggested. Sarah sighed, exasperated. Maybe you should support us in following our dream.

Sarah had a way of taking things over. Take the twins thing in the first place. Fetishizing twins as a conceptual metaphor for codependent lesbian relationships used to be Tegan's thing, but then Sarah showed up and it became Sarah's thing *more*. Okay, so maybe Tegan couldn't really own the twins thing, a cultural phenomenon observed by many, and fine, Sarah had made similar observations. But Tegan had expressed these ideas earlier and more prominently; Tegan should have won.

A more concrete example: Tegan's favorite hooded sweatshirt, soft and gray, worn in, cozy. Sarah had taken to wearing it around the apartment, ripped a *V* into the collar, an improvement, to be honest, but Tegan was still annoyed: Tegan's favorite sweatshirt was now Sarah's favorite sweatshirt *more*.

Or, final example: Tegan's curiosity about animal-tail butt plugs. While shopping online for sex toys together, Tegan had shown Sarah the many, many animal-tail butt plug options available and Sarah had seized on the idea, selected two affordable foxtails, and purchased them there and then. Sarah, who liked to believe that she was adventurous and Tegan was not and that she was teaching Tegan how to be more so, gave Tegan her most pleased-with-herself smile and waited for Tegan to thank her for encouraging Tegan to explore Tegan's wildest animal butt-plug fantasies. Sarah liked to believe Tegan would never dream of doing so alone when in fact Tegan had explored a variety of butt plugs and would continue to do so with or without Sarah.

Now that Sarah is gone, Tegan can be open about this. Tegan wants you to know.

The truth is, Tegan had always been their own twin, fluid and bendable, fickle and flimsy of heart. Deep down they knew this made them incapable of twinning, but they desperately wanted to fit in. How fortuitous that Sarah had come along and made Tegan hers: took Tegan over. Tegan, always so confused about everything, especially themselves, was—at least for a time—solid, stable, fixed, defined with and against Sarah.

Theirs had been a binary relationship. With Sarah as the dominant twin, Tegan was restricted to two poles: precisely the same or the opposite of Sarah. Like Sarah, Tegan had bad body issues. Like Sarah, Tegan had much to say about the literature of abjection. Like Sarah, Tegan despised men and loved Tegan and Sara, though Tegan was pretty sure Tegan loved them first, and better.

As for their oppositions: Sarah, femme; Tegan, butch. Sarah, bottomy; Tegan, toppy. Sarah, messy; Tegan, neat. Tegan, who, embarrassingly, had never been strongly any of these things, was finally firmly defined.

Well, now they were missing Twins Day.

Ha.

> Growth may be hard. But it doesn't have to be complicated.
>
> Step one: Know that every part of growing requires transparency. This means being vulnerable and

> honest and accepting your story.
> The more you accept your story,
> the more transparent you will be.
> The more transparent you are, the
> richer your growth.[2]

The first time Tegan and Sarah kissed, they balanced awkwardly on the edge of Tegan's bed. I like your hair, Tegan said. Sarah asked if Tegan wanted to eat it. Tegan declined with a nervous snort. Sarah said, Oh, and waited. In the silence Tegan realized they had gone off script. They were supposed to be twins, in sync, with twin sense. Tegan changed their response to yes and pushed their mouth onto Sarah's scalp obligingly, gently gnashing until enough time had passed.

> Step two: Create a stance for your-
> self and firmly plant your feet there.
> This means that you must have
> boundaries. You must identify the
> things you will not allow into your
> life because you know they will
> stunt your growth.[3]

When Tegan got home from therapy, the hair was back, now rooted to the mattress where the affected pillow had been.

2. Adapted from John Kim, "How to Grow as a Person (No Matter What You're Going Through)," last updated January 28, 2021, https://www.mindbodygreen.com/0-20798/how-to-grow-as-a-person-no-matter-what-youre-going-through.html.
3. Kim, "How to Grow as a Person."

The strands grew upward, stretching toward the wall. In the middle of the bed sat Jack, head tilted inquisitively, riveted. Tegan slid their messenger bag off, calm. They would approach this as an opportunity, a chance to practice boundary setting. They would make Debbie, their therapist, proud. Tegan had sought out a therapist a few months before the breakup, after a string of recurring bad dreams. In them, Sarah was cast in the role of monstrous femme. Giantess Sarah would be slurping first the front of Little Tegan's body, then the back, then lifting them by the ankle and dropping them in her mouth. Tegan would wake up in Sarah's stomach acids. Then Tegan would wake up for real.

Tegan knew that these dreams, which could have been but were not erotic, reflected irrational feelings, so Tegan had gone to therapy about it. Therapist Debbie listened to Tegan's nightmares and asked probing follow-up questions. Then Debbie introduced Tegan to the pillow exercise, which involved Debbie hugging a pillow to her chest and entering Tegan's space. Tegan was instructed to imagine Debbie as Sarah.

No! Tegan shouted and shoved the pillow back roughly. Debbie lost balance and fell back into her chair. Oh gosh. Tegan was sorry. Strong feelings, Debbie said. Good. Debbie regained her balance. How about "Would you please give me some space?" she coached. Tegan parroted the line and lightly moved Debbie back a step.

There, Debbie said. Sure. Thank you for saying something. I didn't realize I was crowding you.

Now here was Sarah, crowding Tegan. Again. Though Tegan had pushed the affected pillow gently, gently away—or plopped it straight into the dumpster—the hair was violating

Tegan's boundaries. It was erupting from the mattress, thrusting through the sheets and creeping up the wall.

Tegan tried again. No, Tegan told the hair. I am telling you *no*.

The hair rustled slightly but did not retreat.

Tegan reverted to their usual cramp-shouldered pose. Fine, they said. Ignore my feelings. They grabbed their laptop and charger, stuffed some shirts, shoes, and pants into a duffel bag. Socks, binder, underpants. Why do I bother. Zipped it.

Tegan held the door open for Jack, then pressed it quietly shut. Tegan would go on with their life, without Sarah, without all that hair.

Hair fiber is as strong as copper wire of the same diameter. It has a tensile strength of around $1.6 \times 10^{-9}$ N/m$^2$. Braiding creates a composite rope that is thicker and stronger than the non-interlaced strands. A property of the basic braid is that removing one strand unlinks the other two, as they are not twisted around each other.[4]

Braiding is subtle. You do not have to spell things out for the reader. You rely on juxtaposition to do the heavy lifting for you.[5]

---

4. "Braid," Wikipedia, https://en.wikipedia.org/wiki/Braid, with modifications by Tegan.
5. From Heather Sellers's *The Practice of Creative Writing*, Tegan thinks.

The day Sarah left, Tegan cleaned the entire apartment scrupulously, happily. They hadn't cleaned in months, resentful at having been forced into the "tidy" role. They shoved Sarah's sprawl into one piece of old luggage, then two. The left-behind sandals and oversized totes. Flouncy skirts and—balloon pants? Was that right? Who cared. Bye. They stuck the luggage in the hall closet, where they found more of Sarah's things, so they started a third piece of luggage, thought better of it, shoved the quilted coats and floofy scarves, how many scarves, into a garbage bag that now sat slumped against her other belongings. In her previous apartment, Sarah had hired a cleaning person to come in once a week. Tegan was galled to learn of this. But appreciated it too. Sarah's entitlement to indulgence. Tegan could use more of it.

In the kitchen, Tegan fished out the dishes from grimy sinkwater, the asparagus chunks from the drain. These remnants of their last cooking adventure: left there to teach Tegan a lesson. We have plenty of dishes, Sarah had said. We don't need to constantly be washing them. Tegan wiped coffee grounds and dried banana veins from the counters. They cleaned in silence: no Tegan and Sara for Tegan, who ought to feel guilty. For dumping Sarah. For making Sarah dump herself.

Tegan didn't quite understand what had happened. They had fought about whether to stay in or go out, which was a fight about mind reading and twin sense. Then Sarah had talked, so Tegan had listened. Sarah kept talking and Tegan kept listening until Tegan forgot how to talk. When Sarah abruptly stopped talking after demanding that Tegan communicate, an empty speech bubble of possibility hovered in the air. Tegan stuttered, looking for language. None came, at least not before Sarah filled the pause. Do you want to break up? Sarah asked, a threat. They were sitting up in bed, next to each other, not touching. Tegan umm'd some more. You're dumping me, Sarah exclaimed. I can't believe you're dumping me. Tegan made a small sound of protest. They weren't dumping anyone. They were barely there, transparent. Sarah kept talking. No, it's worse. Sarah was reading Tegan's mind. You're not dumping me. You're making me dump myself.

She left in the morning. They hugged.

In Tegan's defense, this silence was uncharacteristic. It wasn't *Tegan*. Tegan blamed Sarah. Sarah *made* Tegan this way, silent and diminished. The vanishing twin.

But Tegan couldn't complain. Sarah was the dumped one. She got to be more abject.

Tegan held a trash bag up to the bathroom cabinet and used one arm to sweep Sarah's left-behind bottles into it. The bottom of the cabinet was sticky with their leakage. Tegan sprayed it down, scrubbed it smooth. The door closed flush for the first time since Sarah had moved in. Tegan turned to the bathtub, removed rings of grime, chalky bath-bomb residue, spidery strands from the walls, the damp nest from the drain; disinfected the whole scene. Then they took a shower.

Now that Sarah was gone, Tegan could indulge: in this newly clean apartment, this big bed, all theirs, theirs, theirs. Tegan stretched out in it, centered. Tegan could be bigger, fuller. Could have big feelings. Could expand.

Ha ha—

Tegan went on with their life, ignoring a new email from Sarah and sleeping fitfully on the couch. They prepped for their Gender and Horror class, went to the barber for a fresh cut. Came home to find Jack scratching at the bedroom door, mewling inconsolably.

Stop it, Jack. No.

Jack kept scratching.

Tegan made coffee. Tegan worked from the kitchen table, diligently ignoring the hair. They felt it important to stay busy if only to support the content of their drafts of emails unsent. *Sorry I'm just writing back now. I have been very busy.* In the six months since she had left, Sarah had sent a steady stream of emails and text messages. In none of them had she mentioned her left-behind stuff, instead presenting the apologies Tegan needed to make. Her emails were a litany. If only Tegan would apologize for these wrongs, then Sarah could forgive them and—they could get back together.

Tegan did not want to do that. They had replied just once: *I need space*, and were proud for not apologizing for it. Given the smallness of the city and department they shared, Tegan was fortunate they hadn't run into each other, except once or twice, okay, five times, none of which counted because Tegan had pretended not to see Sarah. Tegan had actually fled.

Jack chirped.

What is it, Jack.

Then Tegan heard pouncing, paws scraping at the floor. Jack's smacking-mouth sounds.

In the hallway, Tegan found Jack chewing on strands. A few fingers of hair peeked out from under the bedroom door. Tegan scooted Jack away, then took a bracing breath and swung the door open. Jack streamed inside and stopped still.

From the mattress, the hair had grown a path up the wall, around the closet, diagonal down to meet the floor. When Tegan leaned in to examine the trail, they saw it was rooted to the wall. Where the strands met the surface, the plaster became something like skin.

> Human head hair grows at an average rate of up to one half inch per month, or four to six inches per year.

This wasn't human head hair. It was magic.

Sarah and Tegan had always loved magic—they fucked with crystals on chakra points, dressed candles with blood. They kept up a regular Femme Night for drinking purple potions of raspberry liqueur and watching movies like *The Craft* or *Ginger Snaps*. Sarah would transform Tegan with slick eyeliner and midnight-blue lipstick. Tegan liked watching Sarah concentrate, her pink tongue peeking out between her teeth. This was when Tegan most liked their twinship, as dark witches whose bond only strengthened their powers.

But the moment Tegan said the magic words, Tegan was shut out of it.

The worst part was Tegan would not have said those words so strongly or so simply if Sarah had accepted the first story. Tegan wanted to try testosterone, just *try* it, Sarah, see how it felt. Their bad body issues were getting worse. But Tegan did not want to *become a man*, they reassured Sarah. Tegan detested them, too, remember, that was part of their bond. Then why take T at all? Sarah demanded. You must not be trans! Don't be trans, Tegan. Don't. You can't be. I know you, and you aren't.

And so Tegan had to say those words. I AM TRANS. And they came out loud, and angry, and certain. It was magic. Then Tegan was trans.

Now Femme Night and magic were Sarah's. No boys allowed.

> Patient: My hair has started falling out. What can you give me to keep it in?
>
> Doctor: You know what, I've got about a million of these tote bags. Here. Go on. Take it.

Ha ha—

Help.

Tegan wanted to cry. What more can I do? they asked Jack futilely, despairing. I told it no. It's not listening.

At Tegan's voice, the hair perked up, bristling.

Maybe that was the spell. Maybe, like Sarah, the hair wanted contact.

Tegan wanted contact too. Had a bank of unsent emails in which they described that first shot, the euphoria. The sense of things glimmering around the edges, like the time they took mushrooms with Sarah in the desert. That epic feel, the sky cracked open and something dislodging, maybe, new possibilities taking root. They'd tried sharing the bad stuff, too: the nausea and headaches, the bloating. But Sarah would take that as license and argue against Tegan taking it.

*Dear Sarah*, Tegan typed from the kitchen table. They deleted the "dear." *Sorry for the radio silence, but I needed space. I think it might be time for you to get the rest of your things. I've gathered them in some luggage and bags. If you'd like me to be here when you come by, I will be. Otherwise, I'll put them in the front hallway where you can get them whenever you want.*

Tegan pressed Send. Immediately Tegan felt better. They had confronted the problem, survived. Sarah wasn't the enemy. Together they could communicate and get beyond all this . . . hair.

It had crept farther, from the hallway to the kitchen. A wiry layer stretched toward the table. Tegan had been keeping an eye on it in the event that it might attack. In their dreams it had done so already: stuffing itself down their throat, wrapping around their limbs, ripping into their back, drawing blood. But the hair had not made such overtures.

Tegan lifted a hand. The strands swayed. They seemed to sense Tegan's presence, to want Tegan's touch. Tegan stepped toward it and knelt, ran fingers tentatively over the mane. It nestled against Tegan's hand, thick and silky, luxuriant. Tegan decided to trust it. It was gentle and affectionate, this hair. It just wanted to play. Tegan imagined making neat rows of springy coils from the wall hair, a trick remembered from girlhood: take a chunk, twirl it tight, then fold it in half: magic. Tegan imagined braiding the path from the bed, French-braiding the floors.

Maybe, Tegan thought, when Sarah came by and saw all these braids, she would remember who Tegan was: not some entitled dude bro, but girlish in their own way. Tegan giggled, appreciated ornament. Tegan was playful and fun. Tegan had a long history of girlhood that couldn't be erased. This wash of new hormones wouldn't change that. Would it?

Tegan felt a welt of pressure—the strands were wrapping around their wrist. Tegan jerked their forearm back, ripping them from their roots. The hair fell back on the floor, limp and lifeless. Dead.

Ding, went their email. Sarah had responded.

*That's it? Wow. Fine. I didn't realize I had left anything but thanks, I guess. I'll be by tomorrow at three. I don't care if you're there. It doesn't have to be a big deal.*

*PS: I know you'll leave it outside because you're a massive control freak who's terrified of contact, but if you maybe just maybe decide to be home, it might be cool to see you.*

Tegan was *not* a massive control freak. They were *not* terrified of contact. Not-me, not-me, they thought.

If they left the luggage outside, it would confirm Sarah's prediction. If they did not, it would prove Sarah wrong. But that was Sarah's bait. She had baited them.

Tegan needed to think. Sidestepping the hair trail, they made a hummus-and-cucumber sandwich, pulling slices from a thick loaf of meaty bread. When Tegan bit into it, they met strands of hair. They lodged in Tegan's teeth, pulled against their lips, squeaking like a sour string instrument.

At the far end of the kitchen, Jack jerked across the floor with urgency. He had snacked on the hair, now had trouble shitting it out. Long threads extended from his anus.

*I'll be here*, Tegan wrote, then hesitated, imagining Sarah walking in and examining their facial structure, cringing at their voice.

You've changed, Sarah would say. No, I haven't, Tegan would retort. I'm the same, just different. Can't I be both? Let me be both.

Or Tegan would thrust an arm out. Yep! See? Very hairy.

*You should know I've been taking T for a few months now. I ask that you not comment negatively on the changes.*

Tegan was being a control freak.

They selected all and deleted. *OK!* they wrote, and left it at that.

The word "chaetophobia" is derived from Greek *khaite*, which means "loose flowing hair," and *phobos*, meaning "aversion" or "fear." Other names used for the phobia include "trichopathophobia," where *tricho* is Greek for "hair" and *patho* for "disease." Thus trichopathophobia means extreme "fear of hair disease," which causes a person to be afraid of going bald or developing scalp or hair issues.

In the case of chaetophobia, the feeling of lack of control is intense every time the individual has to face the hair. Possible symptoms may include a feeling of panic, feeling of terror, feeling of dread, rapid heartbeat, shortness of breath, trembling, anxiety, sweating, nausea, dry mouth, inability to articulate words or sentences, and/or taking extreme avoidance measures.

A woman is gardening when she digs up a hairy toe. She brings it in the house and plops it in her simmering soup: this hairy toe will make a delicious addition. She's right. Best meal in a while. When she goes to bed that night, she hears the wind moaning and groaning and then she hears a hollow voice. Where is my hair-r-r-y to-o-e? the voice demands. She creeps farther under the covers. She pretends she can't hear it.

Tegan woke to a grazing sensation and slowly opened their eyes. A chunk of hair had dropped down from the ceiling and swung rhythmically across their cheek.

Tegan scrambled upright. Overnight the hair had overtaken the living room. Thick waves pressed against the walls. It gathered in corners, under the bellies of radiators. The couch looked like a Chia Pet. Hair spilled from the bookshelves, unfurled from picture frames. Strands swayed in the air and reached out for Tegan. When Tegan shifted, they swiveled like periscopes.

It could be so easy, Tegan thought. They could let themselves be wrapped up in it, cocooned, taken over. In hiding, they could change and grow, then burst back to life remade.

Stretching up from the floor, the strands squirmed around Tegan's ankles, grazed Tegan's calves. The hair did not want to support Tegan's growth. It wanted to restrain them. Make Tegan stay stuck.

Tegan lifted a knee and stomped. You're not going to get me. You're not going to get me. Tegan sounded like that early 2000s song by the Russian girl band t.A.T.u. who presented themselves as lesbians and could have been twins but were neither. Key difference: the original lyrics were "us," not "me." Tegan had successfully individuated.

Sarah would be by in an hour. In the kitchen, Tegan pulled a drawer handle. Bound by the hair, it opened only slightly, enough for Tegan to reach in and slide out the bread knife, the closest thing to a saw they owned.

They started with the couch. After sawing off as much as they could, Tegan located the new razor they'd purchased and used it to shave the rest.

Thirty minutes. More like forty-five; Sarah was always late. Tegan took stock of the apartment. The hair was still growing. Stubble spread along the walls, tracing a path across the kitchen floor.

This wasn't working. There wasn't time.

Think, Tegan, think.

The source of any hair problem lies at the root.

Tegan tracked the hair back to the bedroom, hacking away strands as they reached for them. On the other side of the bed, in an area unaffected by the hair, was Tegan's desk chair. They collapsed into it, frowning at the hair's origin point. In the corner of the mattress, the bed was distended, bloated with some . . . lump. It looked uncomfortable, sad. It looked sorry.

I'm sorry, okay? Sarah had cried. I'm sorry. I'm freaking out.

Tegan's mind flashed to an image of Sarah scrambling across the bed to perch in that corner, on top of the pillows, sobbing. Her voice defensive, not apologetic. Sarah was freaking out? Tegan was freaking out. Had been freaking out for years.

I don't want to be straight, Sarah moaned. I don't want to be in a straight relationship.

Did Sarah know Tegan at all? They'd always be a big— Tegan wanted to say "perv," but with Sarah, Tegan had been unadventurous. Still, Tegan was perplexed. I don't want to be in a straight relationship either, they said. They were still trying to twin.

Sarah kept sobbing. She huddled against the wall as if trying to get as far away from Tegan as possible. You'll be ugly, she said with contempt. You'll get so hairy. You'll go bald while getting so hairy.

Sarah later apologized for her response, but it wasn't enough. They both knew it.

Now Tegan traded in the bread knife for the utility scissors and used them to stab at the mattress. Punch, punch, punch. It burst open. Close to the surface was a dark dense ball of . . . something . . . misshapen by the springs around it. The stench was fetid like wet dog. Dead wet dog. Tegan pulled it out by the hair. It was a big bulb, meaty and matted, the size of a human head.

Tegan held the bulb up to their mouth and chomped. Crunchy. Fibrous. I'm accepting your apology, Sarah, Tegan said aloud. It felt scratchy going down, like bugs. Fuzzy bugs. I forgive you. Tegan coughed, hacked, nearly vomited. Chewed methodically. Forced it down. I forgive you. Please leave me alone.

From the woods there comes a stomp-stomp-stomping as the wind whistles and jerks at the trees. The hollow voice says, Hairy toe! Hairy toe! I want my hairy toe! The stomp-stomp-stomping gets closer. The woman's bedroom door bursts open. Hairy toe! Hairy toe! Where's my hairy toe? The woman sits up. I ate it.

Ha—

Sarah's new haircut was close on the sides and springy on top. A softer version of Tegan's. It looked better on Sarah.

Sarah squinted at Tegan. Look at you, she said, her voice wobbly and unsure. You're different.

No. Tegan glared. I'm not. Tegan couldn't stop coughing.

Have you started smoking? Sarah asked scornfully. Wow. You're a smoker. You've really changed.

Tegan breathed in slowly, suppressing a cough.

Sarah eyed Tegan's abdomen, their bloated belly straining against the soft gray cotton of their T-shirt. Are you okay?

Yes. I am okay. Tegan burped, released a rank odor. They were winning: they had become the more abject.

I appreciate your coming over, Tegan said. They robotically pushed each word out, throat spasming. Cough. Your items are right here. Tegan gestured behind them.

Yes. I see. Thank you for my items. I appreciate it. Sarah made a dramatic show of stepping around Tegan, leaving three feet of space between them. She poked around in the bags Tegan had packed, then moved to the kitchen and opened each drawer, taking out various cooking utensils. Mine, she said, and tossed them in the bags. Mine. She grabbed the bread knife from the counter. Mine.

Then the door slammed, and Sarah was gone.

Ha—

Ha—

Tegan settled on the couch. As they took in the bald ceiling, the bare walls, some kind of mean feeling rose in their throat. They tried swallowing it, but the swell grew insistent, demanding. Tears formed. Tegan was crying. Then Tegan was hacking, their throat opening up and out. They couldn't pull in any breath. Their face got hot, tears spilled out, and they hacked again, a big, shaking, full-body hack, and then, there it was, the hairball, a dense mess, soggy and stinking. A few spitty strands tugged at their lips. Coughing, Tegan extracted them.

# KILL MARGUERITE

# LEVEL ONE:
# THE ROPE SWING

BEGIN>> So they are at the rope swing, swinging. The rope swing is this dinky little wooden seat knotted onto a long rope that hangs from a big, sturdy tree branch and it swoops back and forth over Swift Creek Reservoir, and you can stand on the seat or sit or whatever. Some of the boys even climb up the rope while it's swinging because they're show-offs like that. And there is Caty in her jean shorts and old New Kids on the Block T-shirt, getting hot and heavy with Alex on the rope swing, at least she guesses that this is what that means. They are making out, with her straddling him on that little seat while they're swinging, back and forth, back and forth, over the creek, and the muddy water smell is lifting up to them every pass, making Caty think of tadpoles and crawdads and such.

If the water's not too low, you can jump off the rope swing into the creek and then swim to the creek bank. It's about a fifteen-foot drop, depending on the water level. You have to make sure to jump off at exactly the right moment because there are rocks in the wrong spots and they can bang you up good. And although Caty is a little bit worried about falling into the creek and dying, she feels okay for now with the wind swooping through her hair and Alex rubbing his tongue around the insides of her mouth. A-plus, Caty thinks, especially since Ray and Matt and Brendan are hooting in support, and Caty can hear Kim's tinkly laughter cutting through. She knows she is doing something right to get this sort of reaction, to be bonding this way with her best friend forever who has already had a go with Brendan, and so there is this, like, amazing fizzy feeling in her gut, and she thinks of all the secret-sharing she and Kim will do after this. But maybe secret-sharing is too kiddish now that they are getting hot with boys.

So Caty starts kneading the meat of Alex's shoulder with her left hand while holding on for dear life with her right. She is surprised at how noisy it is to suck face, but then, this is her first official time. Official. *O-F-F-I-C-I-A-L*. Official. The school spelling bee is in two days, and Caty is her class representative. But she won't think about that now. Her eyes are closed, the air feels good, the birds are singing. It's happily ever after, and here's Caty feeling safe and sweet with her boy who loves her so bad, even though he's not really her boy officially. He'll probably ignore her the minute they get off the rope swing, and that's fine because for boys, hanging out with girls is only okay sometimes.

Whoosh, whoosh. Back and forth.

Then the sky crashes open and flashes red. The birds scatter, screeching out portents of doom. Caty feels Alex freeze up and she opens her eyes in alarm.

"Did you see Kim's hair today? Oh my god."

Through the trees blasts a familiar girl voice, followed by a familiar snicker.

"Yeah, oh my god. As if topsy tails are still cool."

"I know. As if they were ever."

Standing back from the overhang, Kim draws hearts in the dirt with a stick and pretends she didn't hear.

Caty heard. It's them, the new girls, the sisters. Marguerite and Leah Wexler of 1611 Harbor Point Road. Caty can hear the whip of Leah's riding crop as she whacks her way through the forest. Caty can see the undergrowth wilting to protect itself and the ground trembling at the stomp of Marguerite's red Keds.

"We're surrounded by morons," Marguerite is saying. "Morons with bad fashion."

"I know," Leah groans. Whap. "I hate it here."

"Dad has to let us move back," says Marguerite. "He'll break down sooner or later."

They break through the trees. Leah, the younger one, the sidekick, lunges forward, showing off her ballet moves. Marguerite crosses her arms over her "Girls Rule Boys Drool" crop top and stops a few feet in front of where Kim and Ray and Brendan and Matt are standing. And now everyone, even Ray and Brendan, is a little bit scared but a little bit excited, too, and Caty is distracted, her palms gone sweaty and her grip on the rope slippery because of it.

Whoosh, whoosh. Back and forth.

Marguerite's dark-blond hair is parted in the middle and clipped back with candy-colored barrettes, the kind Caty can never get to stay in or sit right in the first place. But Marguerite knows these things, they come second nature, along with her evil demeanor. Hey, look at that. Marguerite's evil *demeanor* is *demeaning*, *mean*, and *demon*-like, all at the same time. Caty is going to win the spelling bee if it kills her, but this is unfortunately only a momentary respite, *R-E-S-P-I-T-E*, from the nagging fear that Marguerite is almost definitely about to ruin everyone's lives again.

Marguerite saunters to the edge of the overhang and puts her hands on her hips while she watches Caty and Alex swing back and forth, back and forth, and Caty just knows she is thinking of doing something mean. But then Ray, who probably wants to get on the rope swing with Leah, gives Caty and Alex the "Time's up" yell. They hop off carefully, first Caty, then Alex.

By now, Marguerite is busy bragging about her older boyfriend in New Jersey, and Caty is safe. Good. It's time for her afternoon snack. Lunch at school is so early. So she grabs her bologna-and-cheese sandwich from her backpack and sits down on the tree stump to eat it.

She is just two bites in when Marguerite takes notice and starts making ugly grunting pig noises just within Caty's earshot so she knows she is making fun of her, but when Caty looks at her accusingly she can shrug and say "What? What?"

Then everyone laughs, even Alex. Even Kim.

And you know, Caty has had a bad day at school and she is sick of this elementary school bullcrap and aren't they in middle school now, after all? She's not going to play dumb and take this, she's going to say something, stand up for herself. So she says, quietly, into her sandwich:

"Bitch."

Everyone stops. Leah and Ray hop off the rope swing, knowing something big's about to hit. For a moment, Caty glows with pride. She has surprised everyone.

Then Marguerite stomps over, rage scowled across her delicate face, and shoves Caty off the tree stump so she is flat on her back in the dirt. Mmmph.

"What did you call me?"

Caty observes snatches of dusk through the trees.

Kicking at Caty's sneakers, Marguerite leans over into her face and makes a low tone like a "wrong move" sound in a video game. "Try again. What did you say?"

"Nothing," Caty mumbles.

"Bullshit, fatso." Marguerite straightens and looks to her sister for backup. Leah skips over, grinning. "Keep her down," Marguerite tells her. "I want to see what kind of bra she wears. I bet it's a grandma bra." Oh no. Caty isn't wearing one—her mom says she's too young. Still reeling from being pushed into the dirt, she protests and tries clumsily to get up. Too late: Leah is kneeling on her shins and Marguerite is straddling her torso.

"She didn't mean it," Kim tries, voice shaking.

"She called me a bitch," Marguerite snaps. "You heard her." She yanks Caty's shirt up over her face and gasps with delight. "Look Ma, no bra! Check out these chunky lumps." Marguerite grabs a stick and jabs Caty's left breast with it.

Caty cries out and tries again to get up. No use. Marguerite prods the other breast, then moves to Caty's belly. Caty whimpers.

"Crybaby," Marguerite says.

Everyone laughs nervously as Caty flails around. She is a beached whale. A shapeless turd. A fat cow. Then Riley bursts through the trees shouting, "Cowabunga!" He leaps from the edge of the overhang to grab the rope swing in midair. Marguerite gets up. "Show-off!" she yells. So everyone goes over to watch Riley, leaving Caty in the dirt to pull her shirt down and breathe deep. She sits up. They've stomped her half-eaten sandwich into a gross, dirty turd. For a minute Caty just sits, holding in the tears, staring at them all as they hoot and holler at Riley, who is climbing up the rope swing while it's swinging, a dangerous, badass thing to do. Kim turns and makes eye contact, mouthing the word "sorry." Caty looks away.

Eventually she gets up, slinks over to her bike, and pedals numbly away.

So there is Caty, riding her old, outgrown mountain bike furiously, all the way from the rope swing to her house, which is a pretty long way, you know, the two being on opposite ends of the neighborhood. Caty is pedaling as fast as her thick legs will pedal, her purple handlebar streamers jerking violently to the rhythm of her legs. She is just one sniffle away from crumpling into ugly-crying-fat-girl face, and she wants to get home before she succumbs, because then the whole neighborhood will think she's a big crybaby, just like Marguerite says, even though Caty has been told lots of times that she is actually very mature for a twelve-year-old.

As she pedals, she passes Kim's house, which is right across the street from the Wexlers. She can't believe Kim stood there and let them do that to her, Caty, Kim's BFF. And Caty knows if she brings it up, Kim will pretend like they were just having fun, why does Caty have to take things so personally all the time? Well, when did Kim get so fake? And why did Marguerite and Leah have to move here in the first place?! Caty bites her lip and stands on her pedals to make it up the big hill.

Before they moved here, it was just Caty and Kim, and everything was magic. They'd go over to each other's houses after school every day, and they'd trade stickers and build tree forts and hunt crawdads and pretend they were dogs and detectives and R & B stars. Then one day a few months ago Caty went over to Kim's house to watch *The Birds* again and found two other girls there: Marguerite and Leah Wexler, from New Jersey, who'd just moved into the McAllisters' old house across the street from Kim. And when Caty walked into Kim's bedroom, she saw all of Kim's sticker stuff laid out on the carpet, and Kim sitting with a goofy smile on her face and one hand extended toward Marguerite, and in Kim's hand was—Caty still can't believe it—it was the huge limited-edition Lisa Frank leopard sticker that Caty had been eyeing for months! And Marguerite didn't even have any stickers to trade for it.

Caty stood there gaping as Kim chirped, "Now you can start your *own* sticker collection!"

Marguerite rolled her eyes. "Just what I always wanted."

Kim didn't get the sarcasm. "Yeah! You can get a sticker binder at Walmart."

Caty knocked on the open door to announce herself.

Kim looked up. "Hey! Marguerite, Leah—this is my friend Caty."

Just "friend." Not "best friend forever." Caty's face fell. She fingered her half of their BFF necklace and slipped it under her shirt. Marguerite took one look at Caty and scooted closer to Leah and Kim so there was no room for Caty in the circle.

It's been like that ever since.

And the worst is that Marguerite and Leah are both just as skinny and little as Kim, and so now Caty is fat, even though she's only fat just a little bit, it's just a little extra, and according to Caty's cousin June, who is a real teenager, well, she says that lots of boys like that, especially when the extra collects in the backside area, which Caty's does, so take that.

Yeah. Caty glowers at the road ahead. Take that.

Caty is being a lame-ass turd, Caty thinks, and decides to turn around and tell Marguerite off once and for goddamned all.

So she turns her bike around, not bothering to slow down, she is impatient for vengeance, you know, and the front tire goes off the road and snags the edge of the pavement, oh no, and Caty swerves back and uh-oh, there is a minivan in her way. It is an Aerostar, going fast, looks like Mrs. Dabbieri in the driver's seat and yep, it is, as Caty thumps into the fender and one of Caty's hearts starts to tremble, and Mrs. Dabbieri slams on the brakes but not before Caty and her bicycle have disappeared under the tires.

Caty has died.

# LEVEL ONE:
# THE ROPE SWING

BEGIN>> So they are at the rope swing, swinging, and there is Caty again, getting hot and heavy with Alex while straddling him on the wooden seat.

And there's Marguerite and Leah, sauntering into the clearing from the woods.

And Caty knows what is going to happen but she just lets it play because she is psyching herself up to kick Marguerite in the goddamn head as soon as she gets close. So when Marguerite saunters to the edge of the overhang and glares at Caty and Alex, all so very amused, all so very what-have-we-here, Caty simply watches, alert. And when Ray yells that their time is up, Caty anticipates Marguerite's distraction and beams her leg out furiously in Marguerite's direction, aiming to make contact with her head.

But all she gets is air, and now she's lost her balance. There she goes, backward, down, off the rope swing and into the goshdarn dirt. Oof, that hurt. Kim and Brendan cover their mouths to hide their laughter. Alex gets off the rope swing to ask if she's okay.

Marguerite touches her ear and looks around suspiciously.

"She tried to kick you," Leah says, pointing her riding crop at Caty.

"Oh yeah?" Marguerite says, and stomps over to Caty on the ground.

Caty sits up and examines her scraped elbow. She pays no attention to Marguerite.

So Marguerite shoves her down in the dirt and plays out the same scene again—or not exactly. This time Leah dumps out Caty's backpack and tosses her ziplocked sandwich to Marguerite, who flaps it in Caty's face, squealing "Eat me, eat me." She's just started stuffing the bag into Caty's mouth when Riley flies through the clearing and distracts everyone.

Then Caty, forgetting all about vengeance, spits out the sandwich and sits up, brushing herself off slowly in an attempt to regain her dignity. Sniffling, she walks back to the trail to her bike.

By the time she gets there, her embarrassment has turned to anger. Caty is mad at Marguerite. Caty is mad at herself.

As Caty picks up her bike, Marguerite's piercing voice repeats in her mind—*Eat me, eat me*. It reminds her of the recurring dream she has all the time with the popsicles in the freezer. In the dream Caty opens the freezer door and all of the popsicles, there are lots, all different colors, the freezer is full of popsicles, and they all shriek at her, "Eat me, eat me," and the pitch of their voices gets higher and higher and louder and louder until it's unbearable and Caty wakes in a sweat thinking her eardrums are shattered and the popsicles will kill her for sure. The popsicles, the popsicles, they scream and scream. And Caty, now sitting on her bike with crumple-face, wonders why doesn't she ever just slam the freezer door shut, why does she just stand there and let the popsicles scream and scream, why does she let them do that?

Shut the door on the popsicles, Caty. Shut the goddamn bitch-ass door once and for goddamn all, motherfucker.

Caty sets down her bike. She balls up her fists and turns heel, marching back to the clearing. She hides behind a tree and listens to Kim and Marguerite practice The Ugly Song on Brendan. "You ugly. You ugly. Yo momma say you ugly." But everyone knows Brendan isn't really ugly and actually Kim has kind of a thing for him and she and Marguerite are just flirting while Leah and Ray swing on the rope swing, whoosh, whoosh, back and forth over the creek.

"No, fathead, you don't clap there."

Marguerite is being loud and bossy as usual. But, Caty thinks from her spy position, we'll see how loud and bossy she is when Caty explodes through the woods to obliterate her. Caty's hands are sweating. Should she?

"U. G. L. Y. You ain't got no alibi."

Shut the freezer door! Caty zooms forward and pushes Marguerite down into the dirt. Kim backs away. As Marguerite tries to get up, Caty grabs her hair and yanks with all her strength. Marguerite shrieks and pulls Caty's legs out from under her. Caty falls, oof, on her bum, but manages to recover before Marguerite does. Then whoosh. Leah and Ray swing past. Marguerite rises with murderous intent as the rope returns. Panicking, Caty catches the bottom knot and grabs on.

Now Caty is whooshing over Swift Creek, her body dangling precariously in the damp autumn air, arms aching, grip slipping, it's hard, so hard to hold on, and oops, there goes Caty into Swift Creek Reservoir, dropped at a very wrong place to be dropped. She hits her head on a rock and one of her hearts explodes.

Caty has died.

# LEVEL ONE:
# THE ROPE SWING

BEGIN>> Caty is at the mouth of the trail, thinking how she only has one life left, but lucky for her she's getting the hang of this. So she balls up her fists and turns heel, marching back to the rope swing like she means business. Some yards away from the clearing, she takes cover behind a tree and watches Kim and Marguerite sing The Ugly Song at Brendan.

"U. G. L. Y . . ."

Caty is about to make her move but stops a minute, thinking maybe she will pray first since last time didn't go so well. So she looks up at the sky or the heavens or whatever and closes her eyes and prays to God, "God, please let me kill Marguerite and win back my BFF—please?" And when she opens her eyes, she sees something glinting way up in the tree above her. What's that, she wonders, and thinks maybe it's a special weapon sent by God especially for her. So she climbs up the tree quiet-like, trying to hold in her grunts and see, she can't be that big if she can climb a tree, now, can she? Finally she reaches the branch where the shiny thing is lodged, and look, it is a rifle: ➤. Chime! This will be easy.

Caty slings the rifle over her shoulder and slides down the trunk to the ground. She grips the gun with both hands and pauses for just the right moment as Kim and Marguerite end their cheer with their hands on their hips, all attitude, all satisfied with themselves, and this has got to be the exact-right moment, Caty thinks, so she shouts, "Bite me, you bitch," and she shoots and she jumps and she shoots and she jumps again.

Wrong button.

Her cover's blown. Marguerite whips a grenade launcher from her back pocket—What! This is Caty's game! But Caty has figured out her buttons and is aiming at the throat of the grenade launcher as Marguerite lines it up with Caty's head, and Caty shoots, BAMMMM, and the grenade launcher explodes, right in Marguerite's face, and Marguerite disintegrates into a pile of dust.

Ding-ding-ding-ding! LEVEL COMPLETE!

Caty's arms go up in slow-motion champion mode. The world fades out.

# BONUS LEVEL:
# SIXTH PERIOD

Caty is in science class, dissecting a frog with her partner Betty Finch. Caty is wearing turquoise jeans and an itchy sweater, and her gun is stuffed in the training bra she finally convinced her mom to buy her. Next to them, Christopher Smith is popping out his frog's eyeballs and saying, "Hey, Caty, dare me to eat these?" And Caty's saying, "No." But he eats them anyway, after repeating more loudly his "Hey, Caty, dare me to eat these?" and getting everyone else's attention, and everyone's like, "Ew, gross, Christopher Smith," and Caty's like, *eyeballs rolling in head*. Then he says, "Hmm," and belches and waves the smell around the room and especially at Caty.

And everyone is laughing, that ridiculous, freakish kind of laugh that doesn't seem like it'll ever end, and then Marguerite, who is an office aide this period, enters the room and everyone just sort of stops. Except for Caty, who understands the mission: kill Marguerite.

Marguerite hands Mrs. Gill the slip she has come to deliver, then walks back to the door. Just as everyone is going back to their frog dissections and Mrs. Gill is waving the slip of paper at Howard Grey, Marguerite slinks over to Caty and Betty Finch and leans against the lab counter with her arms across her chest.

"Hiya, Betty," says Marguerite. And Betty smoothes her hair and smiles, and Marguerite says, "Aren't you worried Caty will eat your frog?" Now she has an audience. "I can hear her huge stomach growling all the way from Guidance."

Betty looks down at her specimen's split-open stomach.

Turning to Caty, Marguerite lowers her voice. "It's you and me after school, fatso. The trampoline. Be there." She picks up the frog with a paper towel and pushes it at Caty. "Yum." And after Caty takes the frog lamely, because it has been handed to her, Marguerite saunters out of the class-room, her MWAH HA HAs ricocheting off lockers, her exultant side ponytails fluttering behind her.

Something glittery catches Caty's eye. Examining the frog, she sees that its heart is bright red and beating hard and strong. Oh, goody. Caty knows what to do. She picks up the frog and eats it. Ba-da-dum-chime! It tastes like preserved swamp, but in the swallowing she has earned a new heart, so take that, Marguerite, you're dead fucking meat.

And everyone is dumbfounded and then, like, annoyingly hysterical over Caty's public feasting, but it's way beyond what everyone else thinks now, Caty thinks. Mrs. Gill asks Caty if she's all right and Caty just glares at her, burps really hard, and waits for the bell to ring.

# LEVEL TWO:
# THE TRAMPOLINE

BEGIN>> The trampoline is this big old trampoline in Matt and Curtis Wheeler's backyard, and it's surrounded by woods on pretty much all sides, which is why it's so dangerous if you were to jump wrong or get pushed—you could go right into a tree, you know, and your face would get sloughed off by bark. It used to be fun and safe when Caty and Kim were in their heaviest BFF stage, when Kim liked Matt and Caty liked Curtis and they jumped and laughed and poked each other, and the boys double-jumped the girls to make them go higher. Then Marguerite and Leah moved in, and that was the end of that. Everyone got rough and mean, and Caty didn't like it, not one bit, so when Marguerite and Leah showed up, she'd shuffle around in the dirt instead of jumping and getting pushed into a tree.

But now she has an extra heart and a gun. Dressed in her older brother's camo, Caty is stealth magic, and she'll check out the scene before making herself known since she is smart like that. So she goes the back way through the woods to get to the trampoline, and tries to be quiet and not step on twigs, which are always so loud and revealing, especially when you're big like Caty.

So Caty is crouched low a few trees back and surveying the scene. Leah and Kim are there, plus the Wheelers, Riley, Alex, Brendan, and Ray.

Then the air beats red and the birds turn into exclamation points that skip across the sky. Caty tenses. Here comes Marguerite, slinking out of the Wheelers' house in black spandex, handling nunchucks and other ninja stuff, and Caty is like, Uh-oh, and Oh shit, perhaps she has underestimated her enemy.

"Oh, Caty . . . Caty Caty crybaby . . . Are you ready to fight me, Caty? . . . Or is someone a big fat chicken? . . . bok . . . bok . . . I'm getting impatient!" Marguerite whooshes her nunchucks around expert-like and heck no, gun or no gun, Caty's not going in there.

She's backing away when she hears a gentle jingle coming from the action arena. Look, up there, in the tree above the trampoline, right above Marguerite's head, something glittery. Could it be . . . SuperPowers? Caty zooms in—yes. Lodged in a big tree branch is a jetpack.

The game has now changed entirely.

So Caty pauses and wonders how she might grab the rocket pack without Marguerite strangling her with her nunchucks. Caty stands a minute, her mind chewing hard on this dilemma. And the smell of the woods is bringing back memories of a few weekends ago, when they'd all gone camping, Marguerite, Leah, Kim, and Caty, so deep in Marguerite and Leah's backyard you could barely see the light from the Wexlers' porch. And Caty is remembering how, when she had to go to the bathroom real bad, they wouldn't let her take the flashlight, so she just went in the woods, close, but not close enough for them to shine the flashlight on her naked bum; and how they wouldn't let her back in the tent afterward until she'd gone all the way in the house in the dark to wash her hands; and how, when she got back, there was no one in the tent, no one at all, and it was really creepy like in *Unsolved Mysteries.* She'd zipped herself in and waited for, like, an hour until she got too scared and had to pee again (she'd had a lot of Sprite, you know), and so she decided to leave the tent and go back in the house to sleep, they must have all gone in after her, that was it. So she unzipped the tent flaps and stepped cautiously outside. And as soon as she was out they all flew at her from nowhere, howling and laughing and screaming. And Caty was so scared she shrieked and peed herself and then they made fun of her all the rest of the night and made her sleep in the bathroom, on the toilet, just in case.

And she had. Why had she done that? Why hadn't she just . . .

"Caty Caty crybaby . . ."

Caty roars, hurtling toward the trampoline with vengeance. In her fervor she registers little, and soon finds herself snared in a fallen branch. She kicks it, trips, and lands in the wet leaves. Wow. One of her hearts flashes. Caty is down.

Marguerite swings around and zeroes in on Caty as she struggles to push herself up. Marguerite pulls her arm back, then releases. Here come the nunchucks, straight for Caty's neck.

Durnnh-durnnnh.

Caty has died.

# LEVEL TWO: THE TRAMPOLINE

BEGIN>> Caty crawls toward the trampoline the back way again. Leah and Kim are already there, plus the Wheelers, Riley, Alex, Brendan, and Ray, and there's Marguerite slinking out of the Wheelers' house in black spandex, handling nunchucks and other ninja stuff.

Caty clocks the SuperPowers waiting in the tree. They'll be more helpful in this level than a clunky rifle, too heavy and long and too difficult to aim while jumping. Yes, she needs those SuperPowers. But the only way to attain them is by using the trampoline. She pauses, strategizing. She will play dumb, she decides. They're used to that. So Caty steps forward and announces herself with her hands up, and everyone ripples with excitement. She hears Brendan bet Alex she won't last two minutes. Ignoring him, she asks Marguerite with much humility if she can please jump on the trampoline just for a few minutes to warm up, please, so they can have a fair fight.

Marguerite considers. "Fine." She shrugs. "Two minutes. Then it's on."

So Caty steps up onto the trampoline and tests it a little. She does some dumb stretches and doesn't give a crap that they are all mimicking her in their outer-trampoline circle; she's going to get her jetpack, they'll see. She jumps and she jumps and she jumps, and then she jumps high enough to grab the thick branch below the jetpack and pull herself up, it is not a graceful maneuver since she has very little upper-body strength, but darned if she doesn't manage it, and look, there she is, up in the tree in reach of her goal. Caty grabs the rocket pack and tries to put it on. A low blare sounds in her ear. Huh. She can't seem to— Oh. She pulls the rifle out of her bra and stashes it in a bird's nest, then tries the jetpack again: 𝅘. Chime! Caty finds herself angling forward while the chatter below speeds up to match the accelerated soundtrack tempo. Now Caty is a SuperRocketrix, and Marguerite is in big trouble.

Caty glances down to see the enemy scrambling onto the trampoline, huffing and puffing like one of the indignant blowfish in Caty's brother's collection of dead fish and sharks.

Marguerite glares up at her. Caty grins from her tree branch, raises a fist, and she's off and zooming away. First she tries out SuperSpeed, then SuperSomersaults. She practices landing by stomping on clouds, unleashing tufts of white fuzz that rain down on her enemies.

It's time.

Swerving away from Marguerite's flying nunchucks, Caty zooms down and lands in a somersault on the trampoline, the impact leaving Marguerite off-balance so she falls hard on her backside. Marguerite bounces on the trampoline once, twice, three times, and Caty's back in the air demonstrating her SuperSpeed aerial moves.

Marguerite manages to get herself upright again. "Come down and fight, you fathead!" she screams.

"Why don't you come up here?" Caty taunts.

The crowd roars. Marguerite spouts samurai stars from

her mouth and Caty dives in and out of clouds to avoid them.

Enough with the defense. Shut the freezer door! Caty folds herself into a SuperTorpedo and zings toward Marguerite, fist-first, kerplow, right in that precious mean face. Marguerite's eyes tremble as Caty's knuckles drive into them.

Marguerite is down.

Caty regroups. Her body flickers as she flies up and into a SuperSomersault and then THUNK, she lands powerfully, knees down on Marguerite's head, which ruptures on impact, leaking all of the slimy spaghetti strands that were her thoughts and feelings.

Ding-ding-ding-ding! LEVEL COMPLETE.

Caty throws her arms up in champion mode, relishing her easy win and the proud look on Alex's face as he cheers for her, for Caty, and even mouths "I love you" as Kim looks on approvingly. So she is totally not ready for Leah, who comes flying at her, trying to slice Caty's face with her fingernails. The world fades out in time.

# BONUS LEVEL:
# AT HOME

At home, Caty eats her dinner and her dessert, and tries to persuade her mom to drive her to school tomorrow because she is afraid of the bus stop but she *has* to go to school because it's the spelling bee, and she cries into her brownie when her mom says no. Why is Caty so upset, Caty's mother asks, and Caty blubbers about the mean girls in the neighborhood wanting to destroy her. "Don't be so dramatic," Caty's mom tells her. "Fine, I'll drive you. Have another brownie." She turns up the TV volume.

Caty marches over to the kitchen counter where the brownie pan is, and look, a slick red heart is beating thu-thump in the middle of the pan. Caty claws it out of the pan and swallows it. Ba-da-dum-chime! New life.

# LEVEL THREE:
# THE SPELLING BEE

BEGIN>> The day of reckoning. Caty is about to face off with Marguerite, Ray, and six other spelling-bee contestants, three from each grade. Caty has worn a skirt for the occasion and is hiding the jetpack under a hooded sweatshirt.

As the student body floods the cafeteria, the nine contestants take seats at the front of the room. The other students sit on plastic circles and impatiently turn this way and that, bumping into one another on purpose. The judges, Ms. Moore and Mr. Smith, are seated behind a table to face the contestants.

The cafeteria stoplight turns red and bleats a loud siren noise, silencing the room. The contestants are introduced. Marguerite's applause is twice as loud as everyone else's. At this, Caty scowls.

The bee begins.

Sixth-grader Harvey Jones is out first, after skipping the second *d* in "hundredth." Then Ray on "subtle," and Troy Li on "schism." Caty flies through without difficulty. "Suffice." "Judgment." "Aptitude." No sweat.

Time is moving rapidly. The game seems to be speeding up. Pretty soon it's just Caty and Marguerite at the front of the room. No surprise. Marguerite has gotten all the easy words.

Caty glares at her nemesis. Marguerite returns it, eyeballs flashing red.

It's Caty's turn.

"'Liaison,'" Mr. Smith overenunciates. "The secretary of state acts as liaison between the United Nations and the president of the United States. 'Liaison.'"

"'Liaison.' L-I-A-I-S-O-N. 'Liaison.'" Hrmmph. Caty leaves the podium and walks haughtily past Marguerite to her seat.

Marguerite gets "candor." Caty gets "perceptive." Marguerite gets "eight."

Caty is getting pretty steamed at how easy Marguerite's words are. So after correctly spelling "memoir," Caty stomps on Marguerite's foot as she walks by. Marguerite winces and returns Caty's glare but otherwise doesn't crack.

Ms. Moore pronounces Marguerite's next word slowly. "'Scalpel.' We dissected the frog using a scalpel. 'Scalpel.'"

Marguerite smiles confidently at the judges. "'Scalpel.' C—"

She gasps. Caty gasps. Caty hovers over her seat, ready to correctly spell "scalpel" and be in position to win it all.

"I mean, S." Marguerite regains her confident smile. "S-C-A-L-P-E-L. 'Scalpel.'" She beams at the judges.

Ms. Moore and Mr. Smith cover the mic and deliberate. After a moment, Mr. Smith smiles at Marguerite and says, "That is correct."

Caty's jaw drops. Correct? She can't believe it. "Not fair!" she shouts. "This is so not fair!" She pushes her chair back and stands up. "She misspelled it!" Now she's next to Marguerite at the podium, yelling down at the judges. "Once you misspell something, you can't pretend you didn't!" She jumps up and down.

"Shut up!" Marguerite pushes Caty to the side. "Shut up! Shut up!"

"You shut up!" Caty pushes back and turns again to the judges. She stamps her foot. "This is bullcrap! I demand a recount!"

"Caty, calm down," Mr. Smith says in earnest. "You can still win."

"But I already won! You don't get second tries in spelling bees!"

"We have made our decision, Caty," Ms. Moore snarls. "Now take a seat."

"But she got it wrong! Tell her she got it wrong!" Caty is so busy shouting she doesn't see Marguerite pull a spiked mace from her back pocket and swing it straight into Caty's skull.

Durnnh-durnnnh.

Caty has died.

# LEVEL THREE:
# THE SPELLING BEE

BEGIN>> It's down to just Caty and Marguerite with Marguerite at the podium.

"*C*—" Marguerite starts and then gasps. "I mean, *S*."

Caty scowls when the judges give Marguerite the nod, but she is determined to restrain herself this time. She won't be whiny and embarrassing. She'll win the spelling bee either way.

Caty's turn. "Recipe." Easy.

At this point, the student body is becoming bored. When Marguerite gets up again, someone, probably Leah, starts cheering, and soon everyone has joined in, cheering and whooping for Marguerite until Ms. Moore activates the stoplight siren to shut them up.

Caty grits her teeth. This is her game! She should be the popular one.

As Marguerite steps smugly up to the podium, Caty takes a good, long look. Her carefully groomed hair, her tense frown. The visible beating of her life force thrumming doggedly at the thin skin of her temple. This is the moment when Caty might see through Marguerite's facade, see what is really going on under her meanness, summon up compassion, empathy, love. No. Caty doesn't want to. And maybe that's not the point. Maybe Marguerite is just mean. Maybe the point is, who is Caty fooling? She studies the restless room. Nobody cares about Caty. Nobody cares who can spell "scalpel" or "candor." Alex doesn't really love her, and Kim is a weak BFF anyway. Besides, the only way to kill Marguerite is to become a better Marguerite than Marguerite is. Does Caty really want that? Yes. No. Maybe so. Yes. No. Maybe—

Marguerite sits down in a huff. She has misspelled "sauna."

Who cares if nobody cares. Caty cares. If she spells "sauna" correctly, and the word after that correctly, too, she will win the school spelling bee and move on to the county bee, her next achievable goal. She can do this. She's going to do this.

She leans forward into the mic and opens her mouth to spell.

"'Sauna.' *S-A-U—*"

There's a whoosh behind her. Caty spins to find Marguerite brandishing an executioner's double-bladed ax. No fair, she thinks and springs to action, jumping back against the podium and fumbling for the power switch on her jetpack— but it's buried under hooded sweatshirt material. So not fair. She scrambles behind the podium as Marguerite approaches from the other side. Meanwhile Leah rallies the crowd: "Kill Caty! Kill Caty!" The entire middle school population, Caty excluded, roars as one.

Caty tries to yank off her sweatshirt but it's stuck on her head, just like in gym period when she tries to change lightning fast and ends up— Focus! Focus! She rips it off, only to feel several hands groping the shoulders of her jetpack. No! Kicking out a leg, she one-eighties and trips three enemy combatants. But behind them, hundreds of other students are amassing, seconds away from eliminating her in any number of gruesome ways.

Jet away, Caty! Get the heck out of there! Caty is still groping for the "on" switch when Marguerite shouts close in her ear. "Die, you fathead! Lose some weight, get a boyfriend, and die!" She lifts the ax.

Not fair, Caty thinks as it catches her neck. So not fair.

GAME OVER.

*MY FATHER AND I WERE*
*BENT GROUNDWARD*

My father and I were bent groundward and picking up pebbles while arguing in our confused, disconnected way, when from up above and behind us the sword of Hephaestus swung down mercilessly to slice my father all the way plumb from his asshole through to his left hip. Then for a second go it came back around, back into the asshole and down through the groin to sever his left leg completely. The sword of Hephaestus was forged of a bronze and silver hybrid that changed color from bronze to silver to blinding in the light. It was lean and strong, and handled effortlessly as it whipped through my father's ass.

Before disengaging itself from his body, my father's left leg shivered a bit, then plopped over and into the sand. From his pelvis, blood sprayed in an arced line, like water from an oscillating sprinkler. I rushed toward him, sorry for all I had said, and intending to offer support before he lost balance completely. As I ran I saw with horror from the corner of my bulging, terrified eyeball that the sword of Hephaestus was now swinging swiftly and directly toward me. There was no getting away: I knew this, and flinched. The sword of Hephaestus caught me between the thighs and sliced off my right leg, easy. The blade took an abrupt swerve then, the flat side slapping my ass before striking the ground and receding into an overcast sky.

As you might guess, we hopped around screaming as blood gushed out of our hip joints and clotted the sand into crimson lumps. Having always been the more competent in times of crisis, I bent down, wincing at the pain in my sliced socket, and picked up my father's left leg and my right leg, respectively. I ordered my father to walk west along the river. I linked my arm with his and we managed to pogo together, like the elementary school field-day game where you tie your right leg to somebody else's left leg and become a three-legged creature, only we had no third leg to share. All the while, my father wouldn't look at me, not even a sideways glance. I spent the time wondering what Hephaestus had meant by such a mean swipe; he of all the gods seemed most likely to be sympathetic. In silence, we continued to take generous hops by turn, our remaining legs strong as steel, as we advanced toward the closest hospital, where the doctors stitched us back up, saying we were lucky he didn't slice through our hearts.

I GUESS WE weren't supposed to have gone to the hospital, because it made things a lot worse in the long run. A few hours after arriving back home, where my mother stirred spaghetti in a strong steel pot, I felt a strange rumbling in my hip socket precisely where my leg had been stitched back on. My father expressed feeling a similar quake in the middle of his left pelvis. That was when I knew we were to bear immortal children from our wounds. I quickly unlaced my stitches and pulled off my leg, allowing a full-grown god named Meninges to spring out, panting heavily; he had almost suffocated in there. My father did the same with his stitches, and from his pelvis leapt a beautiful goddess named Hysteria, with golden locks, coral lips, and the rest.

Hysteria and Meninges immediately embraced, ignoring their injured parents. My father and I stitched ourselves back up; it's not hard once there are holes to guide you. Looking at each other, we saw our children's mythologies in the other's face. They would love each other, grow old together, despite/ because of having an unusual sex life and an uncommonly high number of shared genes.

IT HAS BEEN difficult knowing my son's father is also my sister's father: it's like in the movie *Chinatown*, with the difference being obvious. For me, this has all been a small if unusually sharp bump in the proverbial road of life; for my father, it has been a wall. He walks now with an imagined limp; his head, shoulders, knees, and toes all drag, increasingly lifeless as the years proceed. But my father has always been a homophobe. The knowledge that his immortal child was born with the sword of another man, and the ugliest of gods to boot, is simply too humiliating. This is what we had been arguing about in the first place: why I was so unfeminine, and couldn't I be normal. I had said I don't like being penetrated. He had claimed to dislike it as well.

We have never much talked about our experience with Hephaestus. It is the elephant in the room, as you can imagine. It's discomfiting to have these scars, like matching tattoos, marking the history of what we most wish we had not been through together. Otherwise we're not very close, which I've always thought a shame. We're alike in so many ways.

# TOMATO HEART

It was a cool day for July, a healthy breeze keeping the heat at bay, and I had immersed myself in a matrix of tomato vines, breathing in the vine-ripe aroma and enjoying the yellow-to-red rainbow of garden fruit, when I saw a man several yards away. Silhouetted by the sun, he looked like an elongated Giacometti until I took a few steps forward; with the sun no longer swallowing him, he was just tall, nothing special. I watched him reach up, yank off a tomato, and chomp into it with authority, the juice squirting out upon impact and leaking down his chin with a vengeance.

He shifted and saw me. He offered me a bite.

I accepted. It was a fireball of a tomato, delicious, its tang flooding our mouths and trickling from our lips down to our chins, tickling our necks, tingeing our white T-shirts pink at the collars. It could have been just another tomato on a vine, stuck there, round and shiny, swelling, waiting to be plucked and eaten, with brothers and sisters just as ripe, just as ample. But this tomato was extraordinary. I'd never tasted anything so bright. The stranger and I surveyed each other coolly as we chomped, and I felt the beginning of something, I didn't know what exactly, take root in my body.

I love tomatoes. His name was Paul.

On our first date we went to Mama Mia's, a Ninth Street

hole-in-the-wall. Paul's idea. They knew him there. I imagine he wanted to impress me with his capacity for making quaint friends like Guillermo and Estelle, the septuagenarian owners of the place. They embraced him heartily and gave me an affectionate once-over with eyebrows raised, I believe in impressed approval. At the time, I was charmed.

We had just fallen into the rhythm of a smooth tête-à-tête when our salads were served, striking us silent with their opulence: a generous array of sliced tomatoes arranged upon rippling leaves of romaine with grated mozzarella sprinkled on top. O! And a creamy Italian sauce to die for. I looked at Paul and smiled. Paul smiled back. My heart bubbled with joy as I plinked a tomato slice into my mouth and chewed. I looked at him chewing on his tomato slice as he looked at me chewing on my tomato slice, and I knew this relationship would last.

He had felt it, too, he said many months later, when we remembered with fondness that first date, the first of many such dates, many such tomato-filled salads followed by traditional Italian dishes and slow walks along the river. He was a talker, oh yes, fond of sweeping declarations and eloquent with his hands; our favorite topics were gentrification, environmental racism, public art, and tomatoes. I love tomatoes. Since the day we met so gloriously amid the tomato vines at the farm, we had been back to Mama Mia's twenty times at least, enough for Guillermo and Estelle to know us and give us dessert on the house from time to time, usually when we were arguing, which predictably became more frequent as time wore on.

He took me back to Mama Mia's to propose. Not marriage, but a partnership. A committed partnership. Guillermo brought out our salads, and Paul brought up that first date, that moment when we had gazed at each other with forks midair and plinked tomato slices into our mouths simultaneously. He claimed to have known right then, right there, that we would make it. We would commit to each other, grow old together. My love, he said, will you be my life partner?

I looked down at my salad. He had jumped the gun a little, I thought. I didn't want to think of such things; I wanted to plink a tomato slice into my mouth and savor its garden flesh. But looking at him looking at me like that, my heart surprised me, thumping like it wanted out, like it wanted to jump right out of my chest and nestle inside his. Our hearts would grow old together. We were in love.

So I looked up and said, Yes, darling, yes, I will. Paul let out a huge breath and reached for my palm. We clutched each other's hands and smiled, our eyes glistening, then kissed each other lightly over the table. I was glad then that I hadn't started in on the male answer syndrome baiting, a game I'd picked up from one of our femarchist friends and grown fond of over the course of our relationship. Paul might have reneged, which, by the way, should be pronounced with a soft *g* because it sounds better and more appropriate that way. Paul always rejected my pronunciation-as-use theories of language. I have to get them in when he's not listening.

That night we had a long bout of civil sex and then we went to sleep. When I woke up, it was early morning, and my chest was rattling noisily. Something felt wrong inside me. I was numb on one side, and my chest was swelling visibly, as though my rib cage were expanding. I must be having a heart attack, I thought. Exciting, and highly unusual for a woman my age—but I have always been special. Then I started coughing uncontrollably, so hard I feared I'd hurl up my esophagus. That was when Paul woke up, alarmed, and started whacking me on the back, saying, Are you all right, darling, are you all right, and Should I call the hospital, darling, I'm calling the hospital. He made for the phone. I batted his arm away.

By that point, the skin between my breasts had begun itching uncontrollably, and I couldn't help but scratch. I scratched and scratched, digging deep with my fingernails until, abruptly, I tore through my skin—it wasn't painful so much as relieving. As I peeled my skin back, groaning, I felt something push at my rib cage from within. I thought, My god, I must have a tumor between my breasts. And that's when it happened; I don't know how. My heart burst out of my chest. It popped through its arterial fence, surged through my lungs and my rib cage, and ejected itself through various nervous tissues and muscle fibers with a final rip through the hole I had made in my skin. There it stopped, my heart, still attached to its arteries and veins, but exposed and sagging between my breasts like some kind of unwieldy necklace. Chestlace? If you will.

Because Paul has fucking weird dreams, naturally he assumed this was one and promptly went back to sleep. After a moment, so did I. When I woke up, the problem had not remedied itself. My chest bore a small open wound, from whence my heart dangled, snug between my mammary glands. I was more fascinated than alarmed—fascinated because my heart, now visible to the world, looked remarkably like a tomato, a tomato whose rubbery skin steadily palpitated with soft th-thumps. When Paul woke up, he had an identically similar reaction. Your heart, he exclaimed animatedly, it looks remarkably like a tomato! Then he stopped staring and looked at me, concerned. Darling, he said, we really should take you to the hospital, with that patronizing look like he knew what was best, and I certainly didn't. By that point in our relationship, however, I knew better than to cry condescension. He would invariably pull out the card that said *I have a master's degree in women's studies and a four-year background in anti-rape activism. What do you have, Christine?*

Fuck you, Paul, I said with a yawn, and got up gracefully. I'm fine. I stepped in front of the mirror to examine myself more closely. Not only did my heart *look* remarkably like a tomato, there was no arguing that it was, in fact, a tomato, and large at that, even when contracted. Indeed, it took great effort to resist taking a bite out of my heart. I gasped and covered myself, thinking of Paul's shared tomato-lust. I must keep my heart away from Paul, I thought, or he will surely eat it and kill me.

I put on a loose sweatshirt and began to feel somewhat light-headed. Well, I thought, maybe I'll go to the emergency room after all. I wrote a note and stuck it on the refrigerator, then left the apartment and stepped onto the street. By now I had a severe craving for a big, juicy tomato, so I thought, why not stop at the local farmer's market on the way to the hospital. There wasn't any rush.

It was crowded for a Tuesday morning, with everyone tossing around barked numbers and bulky bags of produce. I made my way past tables of green peppers, lettuce, jellies, and cucumbers before catching sight of the tomatoes at the end of the market. Cherry tomatoes, plum tomatoes, slicing tomatoes, ah. The shiny bright skin, the friendly round shape, the thirst-quenching blood.

Luscious, I thought. Pure lusciousness.

I needed a tomato, right then, right there.

My eyes locked in on an especially large specimen with a

quirky asymmetrical stem. This, I thought, this is the one. I felt a twinge of guilt at my independent tomato-hunting. From the start, tomatoes had bound us together, and now, not a full day since we had made our commitment, here I was, acting selfishly. But what can you do about severe tomato cravings, I asked myself, except eat a tomato? Besides, you are selfish.

As I was beelining toward the tomatoes, lost in my thoughts, a woman with an elbow bumped into me. She elbowed me right between my breasts, right in the heart. I sucked in my breath and stopped still. The woman didn't bother to apologize, just stalked off indifferently as my blood went rushing to my head. Had it burst? Had my heart burst? I needed to sit down and check without flashing my breasts at anyone. I needed to sit down and catch my breath.

I sat down. I looked down my shirt. My heart had ruptured; juice ran down my abdomen. I reached in and cradled my broken heart. Realizing I was in a busy public area, I looked up, alarmed. No, I calmed myself, no one had noticed me with my hand up my shirt; I had my heart to myself, and rightly so.

Having skipped breakfast, my hunger pangs were intense, and heightened by the smell of ripe tomato. I would need to eat soon. And what more delicious than . . . ? No. I knew better. And yet my stomach was turning itself inside out. So I grabbed my tomato heart and tugged it experimentally toward my lips, finding that its arterial vine had some give. I sucked my heart's juice. And . . . I couldn't help myself. I bit.

Immediately I felt stronger in the stomach and brain but weaker in the rest of my body. My chest hurt badly; pain shot all through. I mustered up all my strength and walked the two blocks to the hospital. The nurse in the emergency room took one look at me, gave me a clipboard, and said, Take a seat. Although the pain was excruciating, I told myself to be patient. Other people needed doctors too. But I couldn't even fill out the application form; my stomach was yawning noisily. What was I to do? So I lifted up my heart and took another bite. The nurse sighed. Well, now you'll need a transplant. Doctor!

I recovered fully. Paul and I decided to take a break. I feel sure it is a permanent break but have decided the decision is his. If it was my heart that sabotaged the relationship, it is his mouth that must end it.

I no longer eat tomatoes. When I see them now, I feel a phantom lurch in my chest. My new affair is with grapes. Cold, hard grapes. I like the white kind, the seedless kind, the ones that look like eyeballs. I like to plop a cold, hard, seedless grape in my mouth and suck and suck before biting and feeling all the juice squirt out inside of me. Sometimes, if I have time to linger, I like to peel the skin off before chomping on the fleshy interior. There's something so vulnerable about bare grapes, don't you think? On the tongue, they practically melt.

# TWINS

ALLISON'S LAMENT

$S$ tephanie,

I ask myself all the time how two people who look so precisely the same can be so utterly different and I'm sure that you do too. For instance how we're mirror images with the same shoulder-length, sun-streaked blond hair, sparkling aquamarine eyes, and perfect golden skin. And then how beneath our skin there is a world of difference. For instance how I'm selfless and caring while you are selfish and cruel. For instance how you live as if you're alone while I live as if I'm two, an us, a we. Well today my therapist gave me this book called *The Emotionally Abusive Relationship* and sis, it's us to a tee. According to the book you withhold love and belittle my feelings so I no longer know who I am. Read the pages, Stephanie. It's you. The abuser. You.

How can you exist so happily while I am fretful and forlorn? In order for our relationship to work we have to respect each other's strengths and roles in the relationship. Respecting my strengths and roles in the relationship is something you do not do. All you do is what you want to do even when it negatively impacts me which is fucked. Remember that time you sabotaged my carefully planned campaign rally because you don't care that I have feelings?

That time you wanted to date Ted just because I did? All the times you get me to do your dishes or homework just so you'll say you love me the most and we'll get sundaes tomorrow but then when I show up you've already ordered with Livia. And you're so sorry, it'll never happen again, but it happens the next time too. And when I ask you to stop wearing my new barrette without asking, you say sure but then you keep wearing my new barrette without asking.

The book says you do these things because creating chaos in the relationship gives you a sense of freedom from the stifling confinement of intimacy. I understand. But Steph, when you behave like this, when you get so self-interested, I lose sight of shared goals and who I am within them. I spend my nights losing sleep and then I wake up and see you and it's like I've never had feelings before in my life. Steph, it's this war inside of me. I hate your guts sometimes but sometimes you're so fun and I don't know how to act because I hate your guts Stephanie but sometimes you're so nice to me and I don't know how to act because I hate your guts Stephanie but sometimes you really love me and I don't know how to act because I hate your guts I hate them I hate them your guts I hate them Stephanie

The book says for our relationship to work, we have to communicate. What I'm communicating now is this isn't working. You have to change. From now on, you're going to do your homework yourself and quit being so fun all the time. You're going to be responsible and I get to be the fun one. I'm going to forget Dad's birthday and you get to say your present's from both of us. You did get Dad a present, didn't you?

What a surprise. See how you're nothing without me.

I know you're sorry. You're always sorry. "I'm Stephanie, and I'm the sorriest twin in the world." I don't want your empty apologies. What I want is—are you listening, because listening's not your strong suit so listen. What I want, Stephanie, is your private time. I want you close. I want to spend each morning watching you get yourself together. I want you to look into my eyes and tell me you love me more each time. I want you to tell me there's no love like our love. Promise I'm who your body was made for, I'm what your parts were made for. I know you want that too.

Because when it comes down to it, Steph, when we work, we really work. Steph, I really love us. How we look so alike and yet are different. Like when I'm staring into my own eyes in the mirror and thinking they're yours and you're being so sensitive for once, you're really seeing me, but then I blink and it's just me. Or I'm looking at you and I try to smooth your eyebrows by smoothing mine, like you're the mirror, you're me, because you are, except you're not. And sometimes when I creep into your room and rub my face in your sweaters, which are scratchy but soft like you, I know we have more than just twin sense, that special feeling and— who am I kidding, I hate myself I'm boring I read too much I wish I were you.

What was that? I have been imprisoned all my life by an evil double of myself and all you can say is you are who you are? Well. You must not understand relationships because in relationships who you are depends on *the other person*. For instance see what happens when I rip off your purple miniskirt and wear it myself. Do you see how fun I am when you're not around? How I'm carefree and spontaneous. How I wear tighter clothes, I don't have to individuate. What. I'm communicating. What. I'm sick of being Allison all the time, the Allison to your Stephanie when I'm the older twin, you duplicate me.

So do it—duplicate me. Now. Move your leg when I move mine. Cross your legs when I cross mine. We are breaking down the wall between our bedrooms, Stephanie. We are breaking down the wall between our bodies. If I'm going to be more of myself, you have to be less. Because no matter what happens between us, you can't escape me, can't untangle. We'll always be collapsed in some strange and powerful way. Nothing can ever change that. Not for either of us.

—Allison

# PLEASANTVALE TWINS #119: ABDUCTED!

$A$llie!"

You look up to see your twin sister standing on the back porch.

"There you are!" she exclaims, spotting you on the lowest branch of the huge pine tree in your backyard. This is your "thinking seat," where you go whenever you need to be by yourself and do some serious thinking.

"Time for dinner," she informs you, tossing back her long blond hair. She grins sheepishly. "And will you help me with math after?"

You smile. Looking at Stephanie is just like looking into a mirror. You have the same long blond hair, the same green-blue eyes, even the same dimple in your right cheeks. But though you look identical, the two of you are very different.

Lots of people think of you as the serious one. That isn't exactly true—you like having fun with your friends. But you also like having time alone, by yourself, to read or write or just think. You hope to become a professional writer someday.

Stephanie, on the other hand, hates being alone. She wants lots of friends around her all the time, and she isn't very interested in anything serious, especially school. Mostly she likes having fun—though her idea of fun sometimes gets her into trouble. And she always counts on you to get her out of it.

The two of you have different friends, different interests, and different personalities. But you are still the best of friends.

"Sure, Steph," you agree. "I'd be happy to."

"Allie, you're the best." Stephanie beams. "Your turn to set the table!" She vanishes inside.

You get up and follow her, grateful for the distraction. You've been sitting in your "thinking seat" for quite a while, replaying in your mind the strange encounter you had with your favorite teacher, Mr. Loman. You can't seem to wrap your head around it. Mr. Loman supervises the *Pleasantvale Middlers*, the weekly newspaper you founded for the school. He's a great teacher, but he dresses terribly. When you stepped into his classroom after school to finish an article, he was wearing a horrible striped jacket—and speaking in clicks and static into a futuristic handheld device!

Heart thudding, you hid behind the door. Mr. Loman *had* been acting odd the last few days, rarely smiling and easily losing his patience. You figured it was stress—student council elections had created a heap of extra work for the *Middlers*. But now it seemed clear that something else was going on. When you finally got up the nerve to peek around the door, you saw Mr. Loman reach up to his head, grab his ears, and peel off his face.

As he stripped away the mask, you could see he had skin the color of limes. His enormous orange eyes slanted up and away from his nose. A series of muscular-looking ridges stretched from his eyes down to his lipless mouth.

You are Allison Starling. And your English teacher is an alien.

*Go on to the next page.*

After dinner, you head upstairs and start in on your homework, unfocused, your thoughts on "Mr. Loman's" gruesome face. Within minutes Stephanie explodes like a blond bomb in the middle of your history book. "I need help from someone who got a three-minute head start in the world!" she sings. The two of you always joke about the fact that you're three minutes older than she is. Sometimes you really *feel* like a big sister to your headstrong twin.

"Steph, come on," you sigh. "I'm busy."

"You promised you'd help me with math," she reminds you, her green-blue eyes pleading. "We have a test tomorrow and I still don't get long division."

"What do you expect?" You shut your textbook angrily. "You've been copying my homework this entire unit!"

"Allie, don't yell." She gives you her most helpless look. "You know I was stressed out when Ms. Brown explained it. If you'd help me out this one time, I'd never forget it for a trillion years."

"Obsessing over Gary Luck isn't stress!" you say, referring to your sister's rock-star idol. But you can never stay annoyed at your sister for long. "I'm sorry, Steph. It's just—I think Mr. Loman is an alien."

Her eyes widen. "No way." She sits down on your cream-colored bedspread and listens while you tell her everything: the noises, the device, the mask.

"How awful!" Stephanie cries. "What do you think happened to the real Mr. Loman? What if he's been taken hostage?"

You gasp. "Poor Mr. Loman! What should we do?"

Stephanie jumps to her feet. "I have an idea!" Her green-blue eyes light up with inspiration. "If the device is the alien's only connection to his home planet, he'll be stuck here without it. So we'll steal it. Then we can use it as leverage to save Mr. Loman."

"Good thinking, Steph!" It's moments like these when you admire your twin's scheming mind. "But that sounds dangerous."

"It'll be a piece of cake. Just get someone to distract him during class tomorrow and swipe it when he's not looking."

"I don't know, Steph," you say. "You know how I feel about stealing."

Stephanie paces across the room, her sun-streaked blond ponytail bouncing up and down with each step. Suddenly she stops and twirls to face you. "I know!" she exclaims, her aquamarine eyes sparkling with excitement. "Why don't I do it? We can switch identities during first period."

You chew your bottom lip. While Stephanie always enjoys secrets and pranks, you dislike doing anything deceptive. "Why can't you wait until you have English?"

"I'm too suspicious! There's no way *Stephanie* Starling can get away with nosing around Mr. Loman's stuff. But *Allison* Starling can get away with anything." You nod, seeing her logic. You are widely perceived as the "good twin." Because you are.

"Besides," she goes on, "if we switch during first period, then you can take my test!"

You cross your arms. "No way, Steph," you say firmly. "That's cheating."

"But it would be so simple, Allie. And no one will know the difference."

*If you agree to switch identities with Stephanie tomorrow, go on to page 104.*

*If you refuse to switch identities with Stephanie tomorrow, turn to page 120.*

As usual, you find your twin impossible to resist. "I have a feeling I'm making the biggest mistake of my life," you say, relenting. "But okay."

Stephanie flashes you a bright smile and hugs you as hard as she can.

The next morning, you dress in the outfit Stephanie put together: an uncomfortably short electric-blue minidress with green opaque tights. Stephanie always makes a point of wearing at least one green article of clothing. She does this because she's a member of the Mermaid Club, and every girl in the club does the same. The Mermaids are very exclusive and consider themselves to be as beautiful and special as the mythical creature of the same name.

Soon, with Stephanie dressed in the striped sweater and blue jeans you've picked out for her, the two of you are strolling down the tree-lined streets of Pleasantvale, California, a town that both of you think is the most perfect place on earth. As always, the sun is shining in a blue sky that's dotted with only the tiniest puffs of clouds. With weather like this, it's even harder to believe that your school has been infiltrated by an alien.

You part ways with your twin in front of your locker. "Good luck," you say. "And be careful."

"Oh, Allie." She smiles. "Don't be such a worrywart!"

You have a bad feeling about this.

*Go on to the next page.*

As you head down the tiled hallway to math class, you hear your twin's name.

It's Livia Grier, Stephanie's best friend. She hurries to catch up with you, tossing her chestnut hair behind her shoulder. "That minidress is fabulous!" she exclaims.

The only daughter of one of the wealthier men in Pleasantvale, Livia is one of the richest and snobbiest girls in school, and you don't like her very much. But you stop and wait, faking a smile.

"Whoa," Livia whispers. "Check out Doris Porter. She can't even fit into sweatpants anymore!"

Although you don't know Doris well, you feel sorry for the pudgy girl. You've noticed that she has clear skin and remarkable facial bone structure. If only she'd lose some weight, she'd be pretty.

Determined not to blow your cover, you search for a catty remark. "What a tub," you say softly, hoping Doris won't overhear.

Livia laughs appreciatively. "Come on. We'll be late to math." You hurry to Ms. Brown's classroom. As you enter, Livia leans into you and whispers, "Remember the plan."

Plan? What plan?

You take Stephanie's seat in front of Evelyn Johnson, who smiles and waves. Livia sits behind her. Evelyn is a snob too—not as rich or as smart as Livia, but just as nasty. Like Stephanie, they're both members of the Mermaid Club. Evelyn leans forward and whispers, "Don't forget."

You narrow your eyes. What could the Snob Squad be planning now?

"Scoot to the left," she whispers. "I can't see."

You can't believe it. Evelyn is planning on copying off "Stephanie," which means Livia is planning on copying off Evelyn. "The plan" is a web of cheating, and you're caught in its center!

As Ms. Brown begins passing out the test, you're fuming. Stephanie must have set up this "plan" after you'd agreed to switch identities with her. Your twin's self-serving ways never cease to amaze you.

Then again, you think, softening, she is the one handling potentially dangerous business this morning. And you did already agree to cheat by taking Stephanie's test.

Still . . . how could she put you in this position?

*If you deliberately fail Stephanie's test, turn to page 107.*

*If you do your best on the test but block Evelyn's view, turn to page 108.*

Serves her right, you think, positioning your test by the edge of your desk where Evelyn has the best view. You tackle the first division problem, deliberately miscalculating the subtraction. Failing a test is surprisingly hard, you are thinking, when you hear a scream from down the hall.

It's Stephanie.

Let her scream. The more you think about being set up as the center of a cheating ring, the angrier you become.

But you hate having these bad feelings about Stephanie. You hear another scream and hit the ground running. You blast into Mr. Loman's classroom and push past all the sixth graders standing at the window with mouths agape. Outside, hovering above the soccer field, is your sister, caught in a beam of light. Stephanie is being transported into a spaceship, caught in the grip of "Mr. Loman," who has revealed to the school his true alien face.

*If you alert Principal Davis, turn to page 117.*

*If you climb out the window to save Stephanie, turn to page 119.*

You are doing your best to block Evelyn's view, ignoring the pencil jabs in your back, when you hear a scream from down the hall.

It's Stephanie!

You race down the hall and storm into Mr. Loman's classroom, where you find Stephanie holding the futuristic handheld device and staring at "Mr. Loman" with horrified eyes. "Mr. Loman" has ripped off his mask and is shrieking mechanically. The classroom has erupted in screams.

Through the window, a beam of light has entered the classroom and is beginning to wander around the perimeter.

You grab the device from Stephanie. It appears to be some kind of touch-activated transmitter. Now the beam of light is approaching you. You scan the transmitter for an off button and find a small, unobtrusive indentation the size of a thumbprint.

Hmmm.

*If you press the indentation, go on to page 109.*

*If you toss the device at "Mr. Loman's" feet, turn to page 110.*

Panicked, you press the button. Immediately you find yourself immobilized within a laser beam.

You feel your body being lifted and watch as Stephanie rushes toward you.

*Steph, no . . . !* You try to yell but can't move your face. Grabbing your arm, your twin tries to yank you out of the beam—but instead gets sucked right into it. Now both of you are being transported up and out of the window—and into the flying saucer!

Once inside the spaceship, you are greeted by a small band of aliens similar in appearance to the alien impersonating Mr. Loman. With orange eyes fierce and unblinking, they stare at you with an expression you don't understand.

"What do you want from us?" Stephanie shouts.

One of the aliens steps forward and speaks in delicate clicks and clacks into another device that must, you assume, be some kind of translator. The alien presses a button, and the device relays in smooth English: "Our kind is in jeopardy. Our planet has been taken over by vice. We need a leader who can direct our citizens to live moral lives. Which one of you is Allison Starling of Pleasantvale, California?"

You stare at your twin, alarmed. Stephanie returns your troubled look.

"What will happen to the one of us who isn't Allison?" you ask boldly. The device translates, and the alien responds.

"We have no interest in the other one."

*If you tell them you are Stephanie to ensure that your sister can live, turn to page 111.*

*If you tell them you are Allison but that you will not be separated from Stephanie, turn to page 113.*

You toss the device at "Mr. Loman's" feet. The beam of light freezes, then jerks forward to grab the device and "Mr. Loman" with it. He shrieks mechanically as the beam lifts him out of the classroom and transports him into the spaceship. You are still catching your breath when the doors of the spaceship close and the aircraft departs.

Your classmates turn to you with pale, shocked faces.

"Stephanie, you saved the day!" Beth Hutton, your best friend, cries.

"I'm Allison!" you say.

"Stephanie! Stephanie! Stephanie!" the class cheers.

No one knows who you are.

**THE END**

"That's Allison," you say, nodding at your sister. "I'm Stephanie."

"What are you doing?" Stephanie whispers. "They'll separate us!"

The translator erupts in clicks and static. The head alien nods. At this signal, two aliens advance. One seizes Stephanie; the other, you.

You are discarded in outer space. You float around for a while, wondering where you went wrong. If only you had made different choices . . .

*Go on to the next page.*

You have one secret weapon left that you have not used.

*If you think the secret weapon is a time-travel device, turn to page 114.*

*If you think it's something else, turn to page 115.*

"I'm Allison," you say. "But I can't be Allison without Stephanie. I won't help you unless you keep us together."

The translator erupts in clicks and static, and the aliens confer. Finally one of the green creatures slides another weapon-like device out of hir belt and points it at you and your twin.

You are alone. What happened? Where did . . . what. You can't remember. But something about you is different.

You smile beatifically at the small group of Xagmari astronauts before you. You are ready to shape their world after your image.

You are treated regally on Xagmar and soon you have rehabilitated the planet.

One day you are reading in your new "thinking spot," a holographic tree modeled after the one in your memory, when your xalamdak, a common Xagmari pet, jumps onto your shoulder and starts scratching at the back of your neck. Huh. You've never noticed that lump. You ask a leading scientist to take a look at it. Ze pokes around in your skin and discovers some teeth, some hair . . . a kind of subcutaneous teratoma, ze says, converting to Human English via translator: "What Human Earthlings call a parasitic twin."

That strange feeling returns, the shadow of some forgotten memory wrenching you with guilt, sorrow, unbearable psychic pain. You think of the book you are reading, shove the feeling away. It's a good book.

The scientist extracts the teratoma and places it in a radiation oven to be disintegrated.

**THE END**

Your secret weapon is a time-travel device shoved into your hand by one of the aliens before you were discarded in outer space. There appear to be multiple language settings: you revolve the cylinder until it reads EARTHLING - HUMAN - AMERICAN ENGLISH. A digital display asks you to choose a date and time.

*If you would like to return to this morning and try again, turn to page 130.*

*If you would like to return to Pleasantvale a week ago, before any of this happened, turn to page 132.*

*If there are always more than two choices, turn to page 129.*

You might as well test out the gizmo that one of the aliens stuffed into your pocket at the last minute. The device is lightweight and ridged, with three indentations. You slide three fingers into the indentations and hold your breath.

The device spits out a horizontal beam that scans your body. Your atoms bend. Your vision blurs. The next thing you know, you are inside an unfamiliar bedroom surrounded by strange—but human—girls.

Club meetings always start at 5:30 on the dot, as soon as Kallista's digital clock flips over from 5:29. The clock reads 5:28, so you've arrived with plenty of time. You grab Kallista's desk chair and straddle it. Meredith and Cassie are perched on the bed next to you, and Jen is sitting, as usual, in the director's chair, wearing her visor.

Most of Kallista is inside her closet. She's poking her hand into every compartment of her shoe bag. You have an idea of what she might be looking for, and sure enough, when she finally backs out of the closet, she's gripping a bag of M&Ms in one hand and a package of Twinkies in the other.

The Babysitters Guild was Jen's idea. That's Jen Thomson, guild president. She's always coming up with excellent ideas, but this one has to be the best. It all started at the beginning of seventh grade. Jen and her brothers would babysit for their younger brother Patrick most of the time, but when they couldn't, Mrs. Thomson would have to make a ton of phone calls to try to line up a sitter. One night as her mom was doing this, Jen had one of her Brilliant Brainstorms. What if parents could reach a whole bunch of experienced sitters with just one call?

And so, the BSG was born.

Besides being brilliant, Jen can also be bossy at times. She's small for her age and is kind of a tomboy. She wears the same thing every day: jeans, a turtleneck, a sweater, and running shoes. Meredith Stills, the club secretary, has brown hair and brown eyes, just like Jen. But while Jen is loud-mouthed and always in the spotlight, Meredith is extremely shy and sensitive. She and Jen are best friends, but they are so different that you sometimes wonder why.

Kallista Kimura is the vice president of the club and is, well . . . *gorgeous*. She's Japanese American and has *long*, silky black hair and a perfect complexion (despite her incurable food habit). Kallista's best friend is Cassie McGann—together they're the most sophisticated dressers in all of Storybrook. Cassie is from New York, and Kallista's an artist.

And you? You're the alternate officer, which means that you can fill in for any of the other officers if they can't make it to a meeting. You moved here from California when your parents got a divorce. Your first year in Storybrook was kind of rough. But you're close to your mom, and you love the house you live in—it was built it 1795 and it has a secret passage and maybe even a real ghost. Honest.

*If you stay here, turn to page 122.*

*If you want to test out your secret weapon again, turn to page 112.*

You race to the principal's office and inform him urgently that Pleasantvale Middle has been invaded. In a few moments you hear sirens! A bullhorn! Authoritative commands! Three officers have arrived on the scene. You rush to them but are rudely brushed off.

"Allison Starling has been abducted by aliens" goes the rumor spreading through the halls as students and teachers spill out of classrooms to watch the spaceship vanish into the sky. But *you're* Allison Starling, you try to tell them. No one will listen.

The police officers take out cylinders resembling spray-paint cans and speak into them. They start spraying the whole school, and eventually the whole world, with forget-Allison-Starling-and-what-happened-with-the-aliens mist. Immediately you forget what you are doing and who you are. You know that something is wrong—you have the distinct feeling that you are not who people say you are. People keep calling you Stephanie. You're not Stephanie. But who are you?

A snobby girl named Livia claims to be your best friend. She walks you home, where you recognize your parents and brother, Kevin. In your sunny, Spanish-tiled kitchen, the fifth chair at the dinner table sits vacant, but no one mentions it. There's a fourth bedroom that appears to be someone else's, but no one questions it. It must be for guests, you assume, and occasionally sneak in to steal clothes that conveniently fit you. All the double sets of items in the bathroom are just extra, you decide, because when someone really needs something, she should purchase two sets, just in case. You live according to this rule throughout your life.

Still, something in your soul feels empty, incomplete.

Years of therapy are useless, and you learn to live with the feeling of identitylessness.

A decade passes. One day, a thirteen-year-old girl shows up at your door claiming to be you. Indeed, she reminds you of you. The similarities are striking. She calls you Allison, but you have no idea what she's talking about. You're Stephanie. Who's Allison? The girl is institutionalized. You think of her from time to time but can make no sense of the situation. Eventually you forget the whole thing.

**THE END**

If only you hadn't hesitated—you might have saved Stephanie!

"Take me!" you scream, hurtling through the second-floor window after them. You drop into the bushes and hit the ground running. "Take me!" you scream again, shaking with terror and remorse.

"Don't worry," laughs "Mr. Loman," his metallic screech grating on your ears. "You're coming too." He pulls out a laser gun and aims it at you. A thick beam of light engulfs your body and pulls you toward the beam that is transporting Stephanie and "Mr. Loman" into the spaceship.

Once you and your twin are together in the force field, a strange thing happens. You begin to merge. Your bodies suction themselves together. It's as though you are swallowing each other whole.

You have been waiting for this your entire life.

$You_2$ are treated regally on Planet Xagmar. $You_2$ decide this planet is a good planet and that $You_2$ will not return to Earth.

**THE END**

"Sorry, Steph." You shake your head adamantly. "Not this time. I'll steal the device myself."

The next morning, you dress in jeans and a striped sweater and head down to breakfast. When you enter the sunny, Spanish-tiled kitchen, you see your mother standing in front of the stove, making scrambled eggs. Your older brother, Kevin, has already wolfed down his meal. He has a couple of textbooks tucked under one arm and is heading for the door.

"Did you have enough to eat?" Mrs. Starling asks him. Kevin's hearty appetite is a family joke.

As you're eating, Stephanie waltzes into the kitchen wearing a short electric-blue minidress with green opaque tights. Stephanie always makes a point of wearing at least one green article of clothing. She does this because she's a member of the Mermaid Club, an exclusive group of girls who consider themselves as unique as the mythical creature of the same name. You, on the other hand, scorn the Mermaids. You think the club's sole purpose is to talk about clothes and boys, and to gossip about girls who aren't Mermaids.

Soon you and your twin are strolling down the tree-lined streets of Pleasantvale, California, a town that both of you think is the most perfect place on earth. As always, the sun is shining in a blue sky that's dotted with only the tiniest puffs of clouds, making it that much harder to believe your school has been infiltrated by an alien.

You part ways with your twin in front of your locker. "There's still time," she says hopefully. "Sure you don't want to switch?"

"I'm sure," you say firmly. "Good luck with your test."

Stephanie pouts and heads down the hallway to Ms. Brown's classroom.

You take a deep breath and try to calm yourself. You have a bad feeling about this.

*Turn to page 123.*

This new dimension is peaceful and good, and its people are friendly and eager to welcome you. No one is in a hurry, and babysitting is pleasant. There are no enemies, only resolvable conflicts. It's a fine world.

**THE END**

"Allison!"

You turn to see Beth Hutton approaching with a smile. Gangly and thin, with straight blond hair and pale blue eyes, Beth is your best friend. She is also a valuable member of the *Pleasantvale Middlers'* staff.

"What's wrong?" Beth asks. Her expression has changed to concern. "You look upset."

"Beth . . . I'm going to tell you something awful and you have to promise not to tell anyone. Okay?"

Beth nods anxiously.

As you tell Beth about your strange encounter yesterday, her jaw drops.

"That's terrible!"

"I know," you say. "You and Steph are the only ones I've told."

Always grateful when you demonstrate intimacy with her on par with your intimacy with Stephanie, Beth offers to distract "Mr. Loman" while you look around his classroom for the device.

Together, you walk to your English classroom.

*Go on to the next page.*

You take your seat while the other students mill around. "Mr. Loman" is writing the homework assignment on the board. You glare. Knowing that this is not an authentic but an alien homework assignment fortifies your resolve. You glance at Beth. She nods and approaches him.

As they step into the hallway, "Mr. Loman" gives the classroom a sweeping glance. You feel his eyes rest on yours for an uncomfortably long moment and sense a malicious alien intelligence beating behind them.

Once he's gone, there's no time to lose. Amid the chatter and activity of the classroom, no one notices when you rush up to "Mr. Loman's" desk and open the top drawer, where you saw him leave the device yesterday afternoon.

It's not there. You check the rest of the drawers. Nothing but paper clips, student essays and—what's this? Your breath catches. Beneath all the teacherly props, you uncover something that stops you short: a file with your name on it. You glance through the doorway and see Beth desperately gesticulating while keeping an eye on you.

You open the file and stifle a cry. Inside you find a series of grainy surveillance photographs of you: at your desk, at your locker, eating lunch with Beth and Vanessa Gomez.

You've got to find that device!

You drop the file and quickly search the rest of the desk. Nothing. But wait—there's "Mr. Loman's" satchel stuffed under the desk. You pull it out and there, inconspicuous next to a thermos, it is: slim and black and shiny, its several lights blinking on and off.

When you pull the device from the bag, it erupts in clicks and static. Oh no! You hurry to find an off button and see only a small, unobtrusive indentation the size of a thumbprint.

There's a metallic shriek at the door. You look up to see "Mr. Loman" rushing toward you. You freeze.

*If you press the indentation, turn to page 109.*

*If you drop the device and climb out the window, go on to the next page.*

You drop the device and climb out the window. Before you drop down, you glance back inside. "Mr. Loman" is rushing after you; behind him, your twin is racing to your rescue.

"Steph, don't!" you yell. "Stop!" You drop to the ground and start running, hoping against hope that your twin heeds your command.

You are almost past the soccer bleachers when you hear a sizzling sound above and behind you. A beam of light is trailing you. Soon you are engulfed.

You are transported into a spaceship. Once inside, you are greeted by a small band of aliens who resemble the creature impersonating Mr. Loman.

Stephanie eluded capture. That's what matters. Your twin is safe. You're grateful for that.

An alien steps forward and speaks in delicate clicks and clacks into a mechanical device that is apparently some kind of translator. When the alien presses a button, the device speaks back in smooth English: "Allison Starling, our kind is in jeopardy. Our planet has been taken over by vice. We need a leader whose unswerving sense of virtue will direct our citizens to live moral lives. We have been monitoring your behavior for some time now, Allison Starling, and have chosen you for this assignment. Now it is you who must make a choice. Willingly be our leader or be cast off into outer space."

*If you agree to be their leader, go on to the next page.*

*If you refuse, turn to page 128.*

You straighten your posture. You're responsible, efficient, well-liked, judicious. You are an ideal candidate for this job.

Your training begins immediately. You learn to communicate in clicks and static. You study the geography, topography, history, and culture of Planet Xagmar, your new home.

Upon landing, your hosts guide you across the planet ceremoniously. Wherever you go, Xagmaris are fighting. They want more land or water or power, or maybe just excitement. You become their natural leader, because the forces you join are leaderless and tired of conflict.

This is the role you have been preparing for your entire life.

**THE END**

You are discarded, left to float around in outer space and wonder where you went wrong. If only you had made different choices . . .

In the distance you see another being floating. Could it be . . . Mr. Loman! You wave excitedly; he waves back. But you cannot control your movement, and your gesture propels you farther away from him. Soon your favorite teacher is out of sight.

You have one secret weapon left that you have not used.

*If you think the secret weapon is a time-travel device, turn to page 114.*

*If you think it's something else, turn to page 115.*

You're wrong. There are only two choices.
*Return to page 114.*

Time travel is frightening. Rushing back in time is like riding a roller coaster backward, only faster. Through the private porthole the device has ripped in the fabric of time, you see stars born and watch them die, you see planets spin off into space, comets come and go, supernovas explode, and all the while you are not even there. You are nothing but pure energy until you pop back into being and time in the tiled hallways of Pleasantvale Middle School.

You race to Mr. Loman's classroom and burst through the door to stop your twin—but it is too late. Stephanie—or is that you?—is holding the futuristic handheld device and screaming as a beam of light enters the room.

"Stephanie, no!" you shriek. Your twin looks at you and freezes.

"Stephanie, no!"

"Stephanie, no!"

"Stephanie, no!"

You turn around.

One by one, other copies of you are popping into being and time in the tiled hallways of Pleasantvale Middle School. One by one, you are pouring into Mr. Loman's classroom. Soon the classroom is full of twins.

You stare at one another in confusion.

Stephanie screams again—"Mr. Loman" is inching toward her with a maniacal glint in his enormous orange eyes. You spring into action. You make for the device while other yous rush to pull Stephanie to safety. Some of you work to corral everyone out of the classroom. The rest of you focus on pulverizing "Mr. Loman" with high kicks and punches until he disintegrates into thin air. Your collaboration is seamless. It's as though you are thinking with one mind.

Unfortunately when you grabbed the device from Stephanie's hand, you accidentally pressed some button. Now all the other teachers are rushing into the room, pulling off their masks to reveal their true inhuman selves. Ms. Brown, Mr. Davis, Mr. Gavin—all of your teachers are aliens!

The beam of light approaches you. It's searching for the transmitter, you realize, and you throw the device at the group of screeching aliens. The beam seizes them, then retracts, pulling them through the window and into the spaceship. The spaceship vanishes.

You cheer as one.

But you continue to proliferate. There is no end to the Allisons popping back into the present from the future. Soon the classroom, the school, the world, is overtaken by Allisons.

It is too much Allison. There is not enough Stephanie. Eventually you turn on yourself. But you just keep coming.

**THE END**

"There you are, Allie!" Your twin leaves the group of boys and girls standing outside the gym and runs toward you. "I've been waiting for ages." You study your sister. Stephanie's green-blue eyes are larger than ever, and she looks the picture of innocence. "I've been waiting for ages too," you retort. You don't understand how Stephanie can think of nothing but having fun all the time. But you can never stay mad at your sister for long. Staring at Stephanie's excited face is almost like looking into a mirror. Both of you have long, silky blond hair, sparkling green-blue eyes, and dimples in your right cheeks. But even though you look identical, your personalities are very different. You are the more serious twin. You love school, especially English, and hope to be a writer someday. You helped found the sixth-grade newspaper, the *Pleasantvale Middlers*, and spend a lot of your free time writing articles for it. Stephanie's favorite activity is talking about clothes and boys. But you're used to having disagreements with your twin. From your long, sun-streaked blond hair and sparkling green-blue eyes to the tiny dimples on your right cheeks, it's almost impossible to tell you apart. Yet when it comes to your taste in friends, clothes, and hobbies, you really are quite different. You are the more serious one. You love school, especially English, and spend a lot of your free time reading and writing. Stephanie's favorite activities are shopping and gossiping with her friends, the Mermaids, a group of shallow, superficial girls whom you openly scorn. But in spite of your differences, you and Stephanie are still best friends. You always have the most fun when you are together, and tonight is no exception. You can't help giggling at your sister's enthusiasm. Looking at Stephanie is almost like seeing double. Both of you have blond, silky hair, sparkling green-blue eyes, and dimples in your right cheeks. But your family and friends know that's where the similarities end. Lots of people think of you as the serious one. That isn't exactly true—you like having fun with your friends. But you also like having time alone, by yourself, to read, or write, or just think. You hope to become a real writer someday. Stephanie, on the other hand, never likes being alone. She wants lots of friends around her all the time, and she isn't very interested in anything serious, especially school. The two of you have different friends, different interests, and different personalities. But you are still the best of friends. You open the door and glance at your neat blue-and-cream bedroom with a smile. It wasn't long ago that you and Stephanie shared a room and constantly got into arguments. But all that changed once you each had a room of your own. When you and Stephanie entered sixth grade, your interests began taking separate paths. But though you've grown in separate directions, there is still no one in the world closer to you than Stephanie, and you know Stephanie feels the same way. You drop your book on the counter of your bright, Spanish-tiled kitchen and pour yourself a glass of milk. You sigh and throw up your hands. But you can never stay annoyed at your sister for long. Being twins makes you as close as any two people can be. From your long blond hair to the dimples in your right cheeks, you are exact doubles in appearance. But that's where the similarities end. Stephanie likes to spend time with her friends, gossiping and talking about clothes. You enjoy time with your friends, too, but you also like time to yourself for reading and thinking. Despite your differences, you will always be best friends. Together you stroll down the tree-lined streets of Pleasantvale, California, a town that you think is the most perfect place on earth. You think Pleasant-vale is the most perfect place in the world. There is no spot on earth so perfect as Pleasantvale.

You seem to be experiencing some kind of glitch.

**THE END**

*WILD ANIMALS*

I rented a video from Facets. It sounds interesting." When Selena shared this with her partner, Ry replied, "Another porno?" Selena had been bringing home lots of "interesting" videos since they'd picked up a small television with built-in VCR from Goodwill.

"Probably. Stu recommended it." Selena met Stu through her grad program, and his tastes leaned toward the perverse and the obscure. He had described this filmmaker, Charlie Q, as a local weirdo, brilliant and reclusive and almost totally unknown, though Stu—here his narrow chest puffed out—had admired his work for years. "I mean, her work. Theirs?" The uncomfortable way Stu talked around the director's gender made Selena think they might be queer or trans, or both. She was intrigued. The video was called *Wild Animals*.

Selena inserted the cassette and watched the VCR suck it inside. She settled next to Ry on the sunken seats of their couch. Marlo, their cat, leaped up and nestled against her thigh.

The video began with a shot of a white wall. The camera zoomed out and a leopard padded heavily into the frame, mottled markings winking. In the center, the big cat paused and stretched its front half; beneath dense fur, its intricate musculature quivered. It relaxed into the crouch, haunches lifted, ears twitching, long tail up and swooping lazily. The camera crept in tight. From the left, a fist emerged, gloved to the elbow in black rubber, and entered the leopard's ass.

"I guess we could have predicted that," Selena said. She was unfazed, or trying to be. There was something odd about the leopard's lack of reaction. She assumed the two images were superimposed.

The leopard pushed back into the fist and began to rock.

"Uncanny," Ry said. "It seems almost human."

The leopard grunted. That, too, seemed human. Well, Marlo sounded human sometimes and was still a cat. The fist pummeled steadily; the grunting found a beat. Marlo crashed against Selena and rolled over for a belly scratch.

Then the leopard became a stallion.

"When did that happen?" Selena said. The leopard and horse bodies had muscled into each other so gradually she didn't register the transformation until it was nearly complete. Astonishing. It was as though all of the black of the leopard's coat had slid into the stallion's calf markings, its mane and tail, leaving the body a golden brown—all without disrupting the rhythm of the movement.

This was a film about syncing, she thought. About techniques of editing. She leaned forward, entranced.

"Horses don't crouch," Ry, ever the boner-killer, observed. "They kneel." Selena still teased Ry about their first date, when Ry had brought over a cassette tape called *Cyborgasm: Erotica in 3D Sound* to play on Selena's old boom box and, as Annie Sprinkle gasped hotly through a cosmic sex scene, calmly summarized that day's meeting of their critical-resistance group. But they were right. This stallion's forearms stretched out unnaturally, maintaining the cat's position. Otherwise the realism was extraordinary. The visual rhythm held steady, marked audibly by metronome-consistent grunts.

"Hmm," Selena mused. "I wonder how this filmmaker achieved this effect."

"What you are witnessing is not a visual effect but an experiment." The sudden voiceover was hushed, worshipful, almost obsequious, and very close to the mic. You could hear tiny crackles of saliva between words. "An experiment in possibility . . . e-ro-tic possibility."

As the word "possibility" echoed in the air, the figure morphed gradually into a tortoise, its starkly patterned shell spectacular. The tortoise lifted its backside to accommodate the slow-pummeling fist. Selena frowned, perplexed. The outdated audio technique would have been laughable if the image weren't so disconcerting. The creature's limbs were too long and too thin, joints weirdly prominent.

"Interesting progression of species," Ry murmured.

"Agreed. Cats and horses, hot; turtles, not."

"I don't know. I'm attracted to turtles." Ry shrugged but did not take the argument further. "But that's a tortoise. Often confused with turtles."

"You are a tortoise." It was true. Ry moved slowly in all matters, was prone to withdrawing into their shell.

The next progression moved toward the human. The flat head morphed to a bald bulb as the leathery skin melted to soft flesh. The tortoiseshell markings evaporated into splotches, more than freckles, something else. At the tip of the shoulder blades, bony nubs, vestiges of the shell? Selena didn't know. She waited for the human to arrive, but the figure solidified as human-ish. The tail remained, swinging.

"We are all animals," the voiceover sounded. The word "animal" echoed overdramatically. "You are an animal too." (Oo, oo, oo.) The echo synced up with the grunts.

The creature lifted its head and spoke to the camera. "We welcome you to new erotic possibilities." Its eyes flashed black and reflective, like videotape ribbon. They seemed to stare directly at Selena, who, shuddering, blinked.

The fist pulled out and exited the screen. The creature quivered, then stilled. Sat back on its haunches, stood up, and stretched, tail dipping behind it. The image went black. "Are you disturbed?" Ry said, reaching for the remote. "I'm disturbed. That was disturbing."

Selena lifted Ry's hand and dropped it between her thighs.

They had slow, rhythmic sex that night, *her imagination so inflamed and swollen she was almost insensate.* Of course they would reenact the scene, Selena crouched and grunting, imagining herself first as leopard, then as stallion, her horse dick slapping her belly as she bucked. She suspended her climax for hours. It rolled out in tremors, a slow growl that felt a little like being emptied out.

"IT'S LIKE IN *The Ring*," she said over dinner the next day. "I've been infected." The images repeated in her mind. She had spent her lunch period researching the film and the filmmaker online.

She found very little information on Charlie Q. An American expatriate who had gotten her (sometimes his) start in Hong Kong before returning to Chicago, Charlie Q had been making low-budget art porn for three decades. Apparently still active but likely working under another alias. The only image she found was a scan from a news clipping, gray and blurry. Charlie was androgynous and wore a mischievous smile under what was either a John Waters mustache or a bad printing job.

The film's copyright was 1988, before major advancements in digital editing. That could be a false date, Ry suggested. Or the morphing may be unusually skillful for the time. "It's not like special effects didn't exist before the era of Final Cut Pro."

Ry was right. The eighties had seen great advances in such effects, she reminded herself. *Blade Runner*, *TRON*, and *E.T.*: all released in 1982; *Aliens* in 1986. If its copyright was accurate, *Wild Animals* had come out the same year as *Willow*, the first film to use extensive digital morphing for Fin Raziel, a sorceress woman who shifts shapes repeatedly onscreen. The technology was groundbreaking for morphing not between computer-generated creations but between real animals—rodent to crow to goat to ostrich to peacock to turtle to tiger to, finally, human being. Selena found a clip of the climactic sequence in *Willow*. A bit pathetic, really. The morphing body had clearly been pasted into the scene; you could see the crude outline. Inferior in comparison with *Wild Animals*, which bore no trace of an editor's hand. *Wild Animals*, not *Willow*, should have been nominated for an Oscar.

She watched the film twice more on her own.

In *The Ring* (the US version of the Japanese *Ringu*), whoever views the cursed videotape dies in seven days. After one sorry week of nosebleeds and cords clogging the throat, that's it. You're dead. There was also a cursed video in *Infinite Jest*, which Selena hadn't finished. She remembered the tape being dangerous because it was too engrossing. Anyone who watched it was destined to keep watching it, too captivated to do anything else, even eat.

Though intriguing, *Wild Animals* did not absorb her in

this way. Nor did it clog her throat. Rather, each new viewing produced an opposite effect. The symptoms of her infection were an unclogging, an opening up. To insatiability. To sync. She felt not closer to death but newly alive, newly enraptured. "Erotic possibility" . . . the words lingered within her as she moved through her days, a steady rhythm, an echoing pulse. She was compelled to plunge her fingers into the whorls of trees as she passed. She caressed the slots of the ATM, tried licking the wings of a fly on her bus window (it flew off). She slowed down her body so her soles slapped the skin of the street in sync with the under-rhythm. It was as though she had developed an additional sense that could sear away familiar reality to reveal its organizing undertow. There, in that other realm, was a rhythm so fixed that bodies didn't need to be.

At home she became a large cat. A black panther stretched out on the biggest boulder. She lifted her head and maneuvered herself up casually, stretching, a nice, long, vibratory stretch. She licked her paw to groom her face, letting her tongue loll out, too pink, perverse. Swung her tail left and right, a thin rope of muscle snaking through the air. She padded toward the couch, dropping her spine, her shoulder blades lifting like fins. She tried leaping onto the couch like Marlo. Her body was too heavy, clumsy, too human; she hurt her back. She scrambled down to the floor and became a horse. Pawing at the ground with a hoof. Neighing. She could feel, at the top of her ass crack, the sprouting of a column of hair. She shook it loose.

Ry was not on board. Selena wanted to bat Ry's tiny head with her massive paw. She wanted to chase Ry around the kitchen and stick her claws in their thighs. She wanted to sync and keep syncing.

Ry did not want to have sex with a leopard, they said, not even a fantasy cat. Selena was annoyed.

Ry was dull and unsensuous, she decided, whereas she was shining and attuned. She didn't trust Ry's immunity to the film—whereas she was inflamed by it, Ry found it disturbing. Ry was such a tortoise. Big and bulky, ready to retreat inside when exposed to anything actually exciting. Selena understood this as additional evidence of their erotic imbalance, an issue they'd navigated fairly well in the past but now hinted at an impasse. Ry refused to sync.

Selena didn't like these judgmental thoughts about Ry and wanted to maintain the relationship. She returned the film.

"What'd you think?" Stu said, with a smug little smile.

Selena shrugged, avoiding his taunting eyes. "It was all right."

"YOU'RE NOT BOTHERED by the eroticization of cats?" Ry had returned home to find Selena watching *Cat People*, a horror film about a woman who believes she is descended from cat people (she is). "Keeping them as pets is already morally questionable. Do we have to make them sexy too?"

Selena paused the film. "This is fiction. Obviously."

Ry narrowed their eyes. "Is this about the film? The other film, I mean."

Selena swiveled away from Ry to show her back. That's what a cat would do.

"I wish you would get over your weird obsession with it. It's starting to verge on an appropriation of furry culture."

"Dude. I'm exploring new things. Don't shame me." She couldn't explain to Ry that her new obsession had nothing to do with animals or sex per se, but with possibility. Rolling back the layers between reality and that other world. Where one could be in flux.

And she couldn't tell Ry about her ride on the Endangered Species carousel that afternoon, how she had beelined for the leopard and mounted it. The leopard's back sloped down but she gripped the pole to press her pelvis against it and slowly, slowly she pulsed. Ry would have squinted at her, frowned. Been embarrassed for Selena, who was inappropriate. Tortoise. As the ride accelerated, she increased her pressure, slid up, pressed, back, pressed, her clit swollen and begging. Beneath her, the regal cat moved, dense and warm between her thighs. It arched its back up and into her and yowled.

IN BED NEXT to sleeping Ry, Selena lets her mind stray. She is sinking a finger in a horse's asshole and rotating clockwise, gently massaging the lumpy walls. The horse nickers. No. Now she is on her hands and knees, and behind her she doesn't know what . . . a fox. Slipping in and out. Its thick fur tickling her bare ass. No. No, it's a dog cock. A cat cock— No. The leopard with its swooping tail, hypnotic, upsetting the air. Marlo rubs up against her breast, purring. He swivels so his asshole winks in her face. She sucks in a breath, brings a finger close, close, then she is touching it. His tail twitches. He hops off the bed. She's the cat now, a big cat stalking her prey, a dull tortoise, basking on a flat rock in the sun, neck out and vulnerable. Cats don't stalk tortoises, she can hear Ry say. The pairing is incompatible, queer. She purrs. Tortoise stirs and retreats into its shell. She noses the shell, nudging Tortoise over and onto its back. She sniffs its ridged chest, licks neatly and patiently its openings. She stands over the wobbling hemisphere, then crouches, rubbing her belly against its belly, her rows of nipples tightening as she moves. Tortoise's beak peeks out; she can hear it rasping. "Hey," Tortoise says. "Wait. Selena." She can't. She keeps rubbing. Then Tortoise is on top of her, holding her down, yes, she's yowling and jostling and fighting back, claws out, her snout slamming against its beak. Tortoise is small and weak, no match. Soon she's back on top, snarling, rubbing, her nascent tail shooting out behind her and snapping the air alive.

# GERM CAMP

I've shown up bright and booming. Berk is in his usual position, propped on a pile of thin pillows, his bed and machinery shielded by transparent material, but we're used to talking through barriers. I sit on the germy chair and ask him how he feels.

"I feel," he searches, "like a bloated carcass held together by string."

I smile stiffly. I wish he'd see an empath to aid in emotional regulation.

"What can I say, sis?" he says. "I'm sick of this." He goes on. His body's done, it's hopeless (he says every time). "But look at this new stitching pattern." Gingerly he lifts his paper shirt and grins at the intricate web. Around the sutures, the skin puffs. "Pretty rad, huh? Dr. K thinks it'll keep the kids in longer this time."

Berk was born with organs on the wrong side of his body. The doctors keep stuffing them in; invariably they travel back out. Meanwhile, radiation sickness has killed his immunity.

"Take me away, Hagrit," he pleads melodramatically. "Anywhere but here." I've let him get started, and now he won't stop. Soon he'll be talking about dying.

"All right, bubble boy," I intervene, and take out my notebook and pen. "Let's try a visualization exercise." After all,

*I* see an empath. Together we're building my inner core of resilience.

"What? Why?"

"It'll get you outside for a minute. Close your eyes."

Berk looks at me dead-eyed, skeptical. "Fine." He closes them.

GOOD. EMPTY YOUR mind. It's clear of murmuring, of pain. Find inside it your smallest, warmest self. You're a bright speck of light, a formless form, a bug of self, contained within the softest cocoon. Your bug awareness is dim, quavering, but within this firm softness you sense a hidden, transforming intelligence. Trust it. The intelligence will guide you. You're biggening. You're beginning. You pupate, blurting with each heartbeat. Ba-dum. Ba-dum. That's you, all new, with gluey wings. The cocoon: it starts to itch, rubs rough against you. Then a thin ray of light punches through a chink in the gauze. The light slices through and touches you. You surge. You realize: you can shed this painful container.

Feel the body fall away, and with it, your past. Your hurt. You're free. Floating free, rising up, stunning, elegant. A moth. A bug. A bubble. A bauble. A delicate orb of light, floating howsoever you wish. So float: away from your body, away from this room, to anywhere but here. First anywhere, then somewhere. When you find your somewhere, slow down. Hover. Where are you?

Good. You're in a field. Feel the freshness and purity of air. Come into your body in this field. Perhaps you'd like to return to your human form. Perhaps you'd like to try on some other form. What form would you like to adopt?

Good. You will return to your human form, before all these fucking surgeries. Be in the field. You're safe here. The sun beats bright on your body. The wind. It's gently loving you. Tell me what you see.

TO THE EAST I see a fortress circled by flying cadavers with beaks. Maybe it's the hospital. Maybe they're me. Dead selves. To the west I see a stream. Beyond that, a clearing and a number of—they look human—figures. I'd like to explore the clearing.

You're here with me. Isn't that nice? We race through the field on the way to the clearing. It's nice to be with you like this. Like we're kids again. But we're not.

I know. But we're not. Too much has happened. To get to the clearing we need to move through the stream. The stream has become stagnant, a dead pool of belly-up tadpoles and mutant toads. Let's play in it!

I am being serious. We stomp and splash and smear slime all over ourselves. It feels cool and good. Thusly attired, we head to the clearing. Look at all the people. They're naked. What are they doing? We wonder at their movements. Upon closer view, we realize they're engaged in an energetic orgy of sucking and fucking. Oh. It's a regular germ camp. I'm enticed. I'd like to join them. May I leave you here with this tree?

The air is heavy and green, radioactive, but I feel good moving through it. My arms are to the sky, my mouth is open, and I'm whooping with joy. Freedom! Free at last! Speaking of freedom, you're free to return to the field. No need to stay and watch. Because soon I'll be approached by several meaty men slick with sweat. Contact! They'll fondle my organ sac and it will be bliss. Then we'll have dirty, sweaty, germy-germ sex. Maybe I'll die. Maybe they'll kill me. But one thing's for sure. I'll never go home again.

BERK BURSTS INTO laughter. I stop taking notes.

"You jerk." I'm burning a bit, but refuse to get visibly upset. Berk and his transgressive desires. In the face of his risk, I'm the tame one. I care about safety. I care about him.

"No!" he mocks me. "You thought I was taking that seriously? 'The wind is gently loving you'?"

But it's good to hear him laugh. "Come on. You had a moment."

"Maybe I did." His laughter fades to a pained smile. "Thanks for trying."

I thank him for trying too. I really do wish he'd see an empath. "Can I get anything, do anything, for you?"

"Nah." He shifts; he grimaces. He thinks, catches my eye. "The one thing I want I know you won't do."

This again. I slide a hand into a built-in glove. "Done."

He lifts his body more upright, wincing. "No. I want you to really hold it."

"No, you don't."

"Yes, I do."

He doesn't. He just thinks he does. He likes to flirt with the edge. He likes to make me, the safe one, flirt with the edge. I withdraw my hand. It's our usual routine.

"Told you." He's won. He always wins. I dig deep to access my inner core of resilience but there's his sour face, gone flat with giving up.

Maybe he always loses. I study the sturdy barrier. The plastic is heavy and rigid, a hard and impermeable boundary. There's no opening to open.

This time I'm calling his bluff. "Let's try it." I hold up my pen and insert it into the thumb of the glove. "Ready?" I'm doubtful the tip will break through the barrier; but with enough force, maybe it could. "Say when."

His eyes flare big and round, and he looks like a child again. My little brother. "Wait." He flinches. "Don't."

I suppress my sigh of relief and return my hand to the glove. The dim heat of his palm is comforting. He's quiet. He seems defeated somehow, and I wonder if I made a mistake. "Maybe next time," I say. "I'll smuggle in something sharper."

"Yeah, okay." For a moment he's silent. Then: "And maybe we can visualize ourselves as giants next time. Or giraffes. Something bigger than bugs."

His sincerity unnerves me. "So many options," I say uncomfortably. "Start making a list."

"Right," he sneers. "I'll get right on that." He twists my hand around for our usual round of thumb wrestling. Back to normal. Whew. With my movements constrained by this bulky glove, he has the advantage and before I know it he's tackled my knuckle. "Got you," he says, his grip tight. Okay. He sometimes wins.

# TRAUMA-RAMA

*a collaboration**

*Some of these narratives are based on or were influenced by my conversations with others about their experiences; some have been written by those who experienced them; some are found; many are fictionalized; all have been anonymized and edited.

B est section by far. Every month Melissa would bring the new issue [of *Seventeen*] to the bus stop, and we'd go straight to the Trauma-ramas. The boys made fun of us but you know they loved it too. One time Eddie pulled me aside to ask what a wet fart was, like it was some secret girl thing, and I had to make something up because I didn't actually know! I guess the word "shart" had yet to emerge in the popular lexicon. Anyway there was one [a wet fart] in each issue, usually ruining someone's lavender prom dress. And there was an early period, and someone tripping and spilling soda all down their shirt so their bra was visible, and someone's dad walking in on them shaving their crotch. The same ones every month, a mortification machine. We loved being unimpressed too. Like, oh, you walked into the volleyball net . . . and a *boy* saw it! Come on. We wanted the most humiliating things imaginable to happen to other girls. —S. J., 28

They were probably all made up—by the staff writers, if not the girls themselves. During sleepovers, we would stay up concocting the worst Trauma-ramas that could ever happen. It's funny, we totally knew the formula—some sort of bodily exposure or malfunction, a cute boy or "major hottie" to witness it, a humorous quip at the end—but we were so naive and, well, uninventive that the best we could come up with was an orthodontics mishap that's probably physically impossible during a sexual encounter that's also pretty unlikely. It went something like: "I was with my husband in our hotel room on our wedding night. I was soooo nervous giving him a blowjob for the first time . . . and then his condom got stuck in my braces! Now every time I give my new husband a blowjob, I'm"—wait for it—"braced for disaster." —C. M., 28

This is an excellent distraction for a rainy Sunday! I've been pondering your email in the back of my mind for the past few days, and really haven't been able to come up with anything showstoppingly/jaw-droppingly/gleefully good. But here's something, for what it's worth: When I was in grammar school, I was speaking with a classmate by the sinks in the bathroom and was so engrossed in the conversation that I mindlessly attempted to follow her into a bathroom stall, upon which I was called a lesbian. So for the longest time I thought being a lesbian meant (a) not being cognizant of the natural end of a conversation or (b) someone who liked watching people urinate. —A. D., 25

It was 1997. The first Lilith Fair. I was wandering the grounds and reveling in the queer camaraderie when I spotted the woman of my horny teenage dreams. She sat sobbing by herself on the edge of a fountain in the cobbled square where vendors were selling hemp yoni necklaces. She couldn't have been more than twenty-two, but I gotta say, it took some brass ovaries for a sixteen-year-old to do what I did next. I sat down next to her and asked what was wrong. I nodded, oozing concern, at the same time stroking her hand and shooting her bedroom eyes. Little did I know, I was also oozing something else. When it became clear the woman wasn't the Sapphic sister I'd hoped for, I gave her a lame little platonic hug and retreated back to our spot on the lawn. As I knelt down to sit, I caught a glimpse of my crotch. It was my "moon time"! The Goddess had summoned forth my womanly essence all over the back of my khakis. The stain was shaped roughly like Africa. Not exactly the smooth lover-boy look I was going for! —G. S., 29

I went to Miami my first spring break in college. One night we were at a bar and I was chatting with a guy who bought me a drink. So I drank it. I started feeling woozy, so I excused myself to go to the bathroom. I was able to get my pants down and sit on the toilet but then I lost my ability to move. Something was seriously wrong. I couldn't even move to get up off the toilet. After a while my friends found me and helped me up and sort of dragged me back to our hotel. I know, my bad for drinking a drink I didn't buy myself. I'm just thankful I was smart enough to recognize something was wrong and—you know, I don't even want to think about it anymore. I wish I had a story about tampons or something. —L. F., 32

When I was twenty-three, I was seeing this girl and every time we fucked she had a tampon in, which I felt was not right, but because I hadn't had a lot of sex and she had, and because she was incommunicative and kind of scary, I decided to make sense of it in the way that we all make sense of things that don't make sense, through rationalizing. Maybe she likes the feeling of getting fucked with a tampon in, maybe it extends the feel of the fingers, maybe she is an ejaculator and the tampon absorbs the mess. Then one night I encountered a tampon in her vagina and it was slimy and gross and I knew with horror that it must be always the same tampon. I stopped and asked her about it but she kept dismissing me, saying I was only feeling the powerful muscles of her cervix, so I shut up and kept fucking her. This happened the next night too. (She was really scary, you don't understand.) Finally I couldn't take it anymore, I was having nightmares about TSS, it had to stop. So the next time we were fucking I didn't ask, just coaxed out the tampon as gently as I could. It came out soaked and shrunken and stinking of stale Band-Aids. We both stared at it, silent, until in one motion she jerked out of bed, scooped the lump from my hand, and ran shrieking into the bathroom to dispose of it. Of course she'd had no idea it was there, and who knows how long it had been there, and meanwhile I'd known about it for two weeks and hadn't pressed the issue because I assumed I didn't know anything. We were equally mortified, I think. —L. O., 26

In college, a girl in my dorm who I was friendly with knocked on my door one day when I was arguing on the phone with my long-distance girlfriend. "Hey, are you busy?" she asked. "I just found out my brother was murdered and I need someone to talk to." I guess it didn't totally register what she said (it was a pretty self-involved time in my life), and I responded, "Uh, I'm on the phone, it's sort of important." Later what she'd said—the reason why she needed to talk—hit me and I felt terrible, but I was too embarrassed to say anything to her about it. Now, years later, if I think about it, I want to throw up. (I've never told this to anyone.) —V. S., 31

Hey, friend! I am excited about this project and looking forward to reading what you come up with, but not feeling up to excavating old humiliations right now. I know you and others find sharing cathartic and necessary, but I don't deal with things similarly. —A. G., 38

Honestly, I have so many I don't know where to start. Okay. So I had this boyfriend who was finger-fucking me once, and he suddenly stops, and I look up, and there's this look on his face of absolute horror, like he's just reached into the Cracker Jack box and gotten a fistful of vomit. "What?" I ask him, and I'm kind of terrified, because what could make him look like that, there must be something pretty wrong, do I have herpes? And he doesn't say anything, but he shows me his fingers, which have some brownish goop on them. I figure I must be spotting—it's at the very, very end of my period—and he doesn't know what that is, so I have to explain THAT to him as well, and he basically doesn't accept it. "This should not be happening," he says. Then he says, "Can't you just squat down and shake it out?" I really can't get him to see that it doesn't work like that, and he goes to wash his hand, with soap and great personal offense. This same boyfriend, I got pregnant with him, and he was pro-life (or whatever it's fucking called) so he wouldn't come with me to the clinic or take me to the hospital when I had a bad reaction to the anti-nausea drug they gave me but he definitely did not want me to have the baby, even though sometimes he would poke my belly and say, "Baby in there." I know it sounds like I'm trashing him, but the real joke is on me, because I was dumb enough to get pregnant a second time with this guy, deny it, wait for him to figure it out and dump me, have the abortion (uh-gain) by myself, make chitchat with the doctor while she vacuumed out my insides, make chitchat with the doctor while staring at a goddamn inspirational poster with a picture of a hot-air balloon on it and some bullshit about "there are no mistakes," make chitchat until it really began to feel like I was being raped by this thing vacuuming me out because I felt it displacing my organs and pummeling my belly sick, the way it happened when I had actually been raped, on a weird pseudo-date the year before, and that's the point when I stopped making chitchat and yelled at her to stop it right now, just stop it, please, and she said okay, and she did stop. This same ex-boyfriend said he was against lesbianism because his sister had OCD and mentioning lesbians or things lesbian-ish triggered her. And I told this guy I loved him, a bunch of times. —J. H., 28


There's not one event, really. It's this shapeless ghost that travels with me, and it takes forms in all kinds of ways and often when I least expect it. There are triggers, yeah, but sometimes I can't predict them. And then I have to do the work of reassuring whoever I'm with that it wasn't them, it's just this thing that happens sometimes. It's this whole cycle. Like, I could contribute to your piece but I probably couldn't read it without going down multiple bad head trips. —S. M., 27

I think that having it fictionalized or not quite right is almost more hurtful than sharing it with people. And it's also almost more hurtful if it were anonymous and not attributed to me. Because I own it. You know? And that's the hardest thing. I own it and it took a long time to own it, to acknowledge it. Even just acknowledging that these things happened to me, that took years. And it's not just me who was affected. Getting a reputation in high school, that's not just me who had to deal with it; I have a younger brother and sister who had to live with that too. I guess I've always thought that I would do something good with it. Like work at Planned Parenthood and tell girls who want to have an abortion it is okay. Tell girls who have been raped that they are somebody. They will become themselves. I know you're an artist and you can do whatever you want but I don't know. This is mine. —J. D., 32

A former partner of mine had a really brutal experience as a kid that she wouldn't tell me about. I mean, she would occasionally refer to it to explain certain reactions to things but she wouldn't tell me exactly what happened. Even though I knew it was a bad experience that she didn't want to relive, I was a little loopy one night, maybe a little drunk, and I made it into a silly game, like I was trying to get her to share some juicy but benign secret, like who's-your-crush, tell-me-tell-me. "What-was-it-what-happened-can-I-guess-if-I-guess-right-will-you-tell-me," I went in a singsong voice, like it was fun. I'm so ashamed. She tolerated me for a few minutes with what I realize now was an embarrassed smile, embarrassed for me, I mean, and then she looked me straight in the face and said, firmly, "No." —H. P., 28

# EARL AND ED

*with images by Marian Runk*

There once was an orchid named Ed. He fell in total love with a wasp named Earl, who loved Ed back, totally. Together they became something else, not Earl and not Ed but Earl&Ed, wherein there ceased entirely to be Earl or Ed separately, although Earl&Ed retained the specificities of both its components.

> Earl + Ed → Earl&Ed
> Earl&Ed ≠ Earl + Ed
> i.e., Earl&Ed > Earl + Ed
> i.e., Earl&Ed = (Earl→Ed) + (Ed→Earl)*
>
> *where → is a form of becoming

EARL&ED STARTED OFF as any other insect-flower pair, each being one of many partners for the other. Earl&Ed met in the full bloom of Ed's second spring and Earl's first and only. Ed was opening himself up for any number of interested insects who relied on nectar to survive, while Earl was slurping the nectar of any number of flowers, meanwhile collecting and depositing pollen to contribute to her partners' reproductive cycles. Though this kind of partner-sharing was performed with both duty and respect, neither of them had any special feelings for their partners.

Earl was a wasp. She inhabited a nest made of wood pulp that bulged obscenely from the end of a hollowed-out log. Earl was a worker wasp. Cordial and friendly to her fellow workers, she bzzz'd as she worked, chewing wood into pulp and dutifully facilitating the expansion of the nest. Earl's bzzz expressed the appropriate contentment toward and resignation to her role in the wasp community, which required also that she defend the nest and provide nourishment to its larvae by paralyzing insects and tearing them apart to transport back to her wards.

*Earl, a worker, could only ever be leaving to feed and find nourishment for the larvae.*

While Earl had spent many days and nights certain that her life and role were decent and worthwhile, increasingly she was beginning to doubt this. Having again and again watched the male drones around her leave the nest forever to mate, with ceremony and adventure, Earl was beginning to recognize the limits of her own life and role. Earl, a worker, could only ever be leaving to feed and find nourishment for the larvae. She was always having to return to chew more wood into pulp. She would be leaving and returning and leaving and returning always and always until her death.

One day Earl was off on a fly, venturing farther from her nest than usual. She flew and she flew, absorbedly contemplating her fixed place in the wasp community and in the ecosystem at large. When she looked into the future, all she could see was work, and small talk, and sameness, until she died when the weather turned. "Pah," Earl was spitting in helplessness and disgust, her mouth still gummy with wood pulp, when a great and impossible yearning came upon her. She had caught the whiff of nectar rushing toward her in the oncoming wind.

Past the anthills and past their ants and past the sewers and their mosquitoes and past the azaleas and dandelions, Earl feverishly followed this scent to its origin in an ostentatious orchid whose showy petals and pert sepals fluttered invitingly in the breeze.

Earl stopped short. Being intimidated and feeling suddenly and uncharacteristically shy but fervently desiring this nectar, Earl hid on a bush leaf to think.

ED WAS AN orchid. Confined to a pot, his roots coiled into bark chips or sprang up into the air. Uncommonly isolated on a shaded patio, Ed had only ants and spider mites to keep him constant company, and the human who intermittently tended him. With the exception of Anyx the Butterfly, Ed's one long-term partner who would check in on him now and again, most of Ed's winged visitors came upon him by accident, attracted by a whiff of his scent or simply taking the long route back to their homes. Ed's visitors, infrequent though they were, brought him any important news of the community, so that if Ed may have been lonely, Ed may not have understood that he was lonely. Ed was content with his meager and easy slice of perennial life, and in an effort to occupy himself kept up a pronounced interest in understanding weather patterns.

*And when Earl landed on Ed's sticky labellum she immediately began thrusting into it.*

Ed, having heard Earl's bzzz from the east, had turned to face the incoming insect. He hadn't had a visitor all day; his nectar felt swollen in his spur. He rushed to straighten his stalk and fluff up his petals, in doing so releasing another whiff into the air.

Earl, on his bush leaf breathing this new scent, swiftly sprang forward with lust. Ed regarded his guest curiously. At the sight of Earl's furry stripes and large and penetrating multiple eyes, Ed's stamen trembled. And when Earl landed on Ed's sticky labellum, she found herself so overwhelmed by Ed's scent and shape, she immediately began thrusting into it. Although Ed might typically have felt violated by such an act without introductions, this wasp felt welcome on his labellum.

"I'm Ed," he communicated, gasping.

Earl, finally controlling and restraining herself, crept over to the edge of Ed's right petal. "I'm Earl," she whispered, peering intently into Ed's center. "And I like the way you smell."

Ed blushed and hid his face. "I like the way you feel," he squeaked boldly.

Earl drew out her proboscis and slowly, tenderly sucked up Ed's nectar. Ed shivered with pleasure.

Earl returned to her nest with vigor.

*"I like the way you smell," she whispered, peering intently into Ed's center.*

OVER TIME, AS Earl swooped in more and more on Ed and Ed opened up more and more for Earl, between them grew a certain interdependence. Earl being practical and affectionate, and Ed being sensitive and affection-starved, they quickly found that each was the other's complement.

Ed, with his impeccable style and elegant posture, would arrange his petals strikingly, and Earl would admire his attention to detail. Earl might give Ed an important weather report, and Ed might pass on any gossip brought in from other insects, for instance, "There will be a fire drill in the nest today," or "The honeybees, lacking resources, are plotting to take over your nest." They would then grow bashful and silent as they conducted the intimate transaction that was Earl's feeding, lingering longer than necessary each time.

Because of their conversational and physical exchanges and their blossoming ease and delight with each other, Earl and Ed began to look forward to seeing each other more than they looked forward to seeing any of their other partners. Each found this curious and startling, with each avoiding addressing it for fear that in the talking, the feeling might fall away.

Then one day Earl swooped in on Ed and found him shriveled up and miserable.

"Ed, what's wrong?" Earl asked with concern.

Ed shuddered, and Earl understood that something terrible had happened. She hovered anxiously by Ed's side and waited for him to speak.

Ed broke down and sobbed.

Not knowing what to do, for this was a new kind of emotional reaction from Ed that Earl had not yet seen, Earl attempted to soothe Ed by telling him calmly about her day. When eventually Ed had relaxed, Earl hovered closer.

"Ed, I'm sorry you feel so bad. Would it be okay if I gave you a hug?"

Ed nodded, sniffing. Earl vibrated Ed's petals with her body.

"There, there," said Earl. "Is there anything you want to tell me?"

Ed, nodding again, breathed deep until he was capable of relating the following information:

Violet the Furry Moth had landed on Ed's labellum in the

night and without asking slurped his nectar with her long and disgusting tongue.

"Just because I attracted her doesn't mean I'm available to her," Ed pointed out angrily. "Oh, Earl, it was awful."

Ed sagged against Earl as he said this. Earl frowned. Stroking his petals gently, she murmured, "Shh, shh."

Earl stayed with Ed that day, and the next and the next. When Ed was feeling better and more secure in his body and world, Earl went off on a fly to find and paralyze Violet the Furry Moth with her stinger. She chewed Violet into pieces and then she carried the pieces to the nest, where she fed them one by one to her larvae wards, who jiggled in hungry anticipation. Although Ed questioned Earl's decision to avenge him without first asking him what he needed, and although the intensity of her vengeance did give him pause, in truth Ed had never felt so defended.

*Earl chewed Violet the Furry Moth into pieces and carried the pieces back to the nest, where she fed them one by one to her larvae wards.*

THE PROBLEM WAS that both Earl and Ed wanted desperately to be exclusive but didn't know how, because the insect-flower community did not support such relationships.

Neither wasps nor orchids were considered exclusive by nature, and those couples who did choose such a path were seen as selfish and abnormal freaks who would orchestrate the downfall of their community by preventing orchids from reproducing and wasps from sustaining their nests. But Earl and Ed didn't care.

And so they chose to be in an exclusive and monogamous relationship, regardless of the certainty of their shunning.

NATURALLY THE PROBLEM was that Earl&Ed was, as expected, shunned. Dromedus the Drone showed up one day to inform Earl that she had been excommunicated from the nest. He did his best to shame her, claiming that her larvae had starved and that the queen, her mother, would never forgive her, not in a million days.

Earl, giddy with love, registered little of this, bzzz'ing over Dromedus in her continued and overwhelming joy. Dromedus, gliding away in disgust, yelled finally, "What you are doing is unnatural." Earl&Ed, cuddling with contentment, did not even deign to respond.

With word spreading, so began several hours of winged insects flying by and spitting on them. Earl's coworkers swooped over Earl&Ed, flinging wood pulp on Ed's petals and hurling insults and anger at Earl. "Traitor." "Flowerfucker." "Pervert." Protected within Ed's strong petals, Earl&Ed quivered with anxiety, whimpering at each lash of pulp that struck Ed's body.

Then the sky broke open and lightning struck. The wasps retreated, grumbling with annoyance. The rain, though hard, cleared the pulp from Ed's body and cooled his stinging petals.

Earl&Ed had survived.

Meanwhile in the whorl of a nearby tree trunk, Anyx the Butterfly had been watching Earl&Ed cuddle in the warm summer rain. Ed's only regular partner for so long, Anyx had been saddened to learn that Ed's nectar was no longer available to him. But Anyx, though disappointed, supported Ed's choices, and watching from afar, was beginning to understand why Ed had done what he'd done, and even felt a twinge of longing himself. He brushed it aside and, when the rain passed, left to find another flower.

THE PROBLEM WAS that sometimes Earl&Ed would need to split open or apart and return to being Earl and Ed separately. Although this was uncomfortable for all three of the involved entities, it was necessary for continuing to live.

The problem was that Earl was mobile, and Ed was immobile. It was always only Earl who could initiate a splitting of their entity and take off, a lone wasp in the night.

Naturally what the problem was, was that whenever Earl left, Ed couldn't also leave. Ed could only be stuck in his pot, anxiously waiting for Earl. Earl always came back, but how could Ed be sure of Earl? All he could do was wait, waving dejectedly in the wind.

Ed had anxiety problems, Earl would say when she returned. Ed needed to trust her and stop being such a worrywart. Ed needed to know that Earl loved him more than anything in this big, bright ecosystem and oh, Ed, Earl needed him so much.

"But Earl," Ed would reply. "What might happen to you in the hard rain and thunder? Terrible things might happen. Your wings might get torn off. You might get blown into a windshield. All sorts of dreadful things might happen, and I wouldn't even have any way of knowing!"

Earl could say nothing to comfort Ed.

And then Ed, always already fearing Earl's imminent departure, always already convinced that Earl would begin feeding from other flowers, if she wasn't already, would be compelled to produce more and more nectar for Earl to take. And Earl would keep taking and taking it.

Ed became the giver. He gave and gave, producing unparalleled amounts of nectar to keep Earl from leaving.

Earl became the taker. She took and took, feeding on Ed's nectar and unable to help Ed cross-pollinate.

Ed gave and gave, and gave and gave, and he gave and he gave until he forgot who he was. He wasn't anybody. He was some small part of Earl&Ed. Who was Ed when there was no Ed, but only Earl&Ed? The Ed who no longer existed apart from Earl&Ed felt bad, and self-less, and used.

On the other side of things was Earl. Earl took and took, and took and took, and she took and she took until she was swollen with Ed's giving, and bloated, and uncomfortable, like she needed to go for a fly. And so Earl would have to leave. She could only take so much. Earl would feel misused, manipulated with nourishment into love.

This cycle continued for some time.

Until Earl, one day, returning from an unusually long fly, looked at Ed, took a long and hard and loving look, and noticed that Ed's leaves were all in a twist.

"Ed, did something happen? Why are your leaves in a twist?"

Ed, unable to make eye contact, could only droop and moan.

"Ed, please. Look at me. Give me your true feelings."

Ed sniffed, and wailed, "It's just . . . I am sick of being stuck here, Earl. Why am I always stuck here?"

Earl paused and considered before answering. "Because, Ed, that's the way you're made."

"But I don't want to be made like this. I want to go with you!"

"Ed, you can't go with me. You have to stay in your pot."

"But it's not fair! You leave whenever you want and I have to stay here and think about it!"

At the forcefulness of Ed's emotions, Earl retreated, hurt. "Ed, where is this coming from?" she said softly.

Ed's face was pained and contorted. "I just . . . I hate that I'm stuck here while you do whatever you want. Why do I have to be the orchid all the time?"

Earl, knowing the answer to this question, brightened. "You're not the orchid, Ed. There's no orchid here. There are no longer binary machines." Earl nuzzled Ed's center with her head and paused, thinking. "The problem, Ed, is that we have no models. Insect-flower monogamy is in the minority, and grossly misunderstood by the community. How can we know how to act?"

"I don't know, Earl. It sure is hard sometimes to know how to act. I feel like I'm just being myself, but then sometimes I'm some exaggerated and flowerier version of myself because I think that's what you want. But do I want to be that? I don't know, Earl. Sometimes I get so confused." Ed started crying.

"Oh, Ed, you think too hard." Earl paused and softened her voice. "Just be you and I'll be me and we won't worry about who we want to be or should be. There is no 'should' here. There is only us. No object, no subject, just us, each of us becoming the other but also remaining ourselves. Earl&Ed."

"But why is it always Earl&Ed and never Ed&Earl?"

"Ed. Hush. If you want to be Ed&Earl, then we can be Ed&Earl. How is that, Ed? How does that sound to you?"

Ed breathed a perfumed sigh of relief and perked his petals up prettily. "That sounds okay, I guess. I guess that sounds okay."

Earl bzzz'd and bzzz'd, and the two were one again.

AS ED&EARL, the couple was again on solid ground. Ed felt more in control than ever, a new and good feeling for him, and Earl felt happy that Ed was happy.

Until Ed decided that Earl could no longer go on her flies.

"Earl, you can't leave me," Ed said, wrapping her up in his leaves.

"You can't control me, Ed. I need to go for a fly."

"But there's no Ed&Earl without Earl. Earl, you have to stay."

"Ed, it's in my nature! It's not my fault you're stuck here." Earl bzzz'd furiously, battering Ed's leaves with her wings. "Put yourself in my wings. I can't take you anywhere. How do you think that makes me feel?"

"That's not fair, Earl. You have advantages that I don't have!"

"Exactly! And you resent them when you should be respecting and admiring them!"

Ed scoffed. "You don't respect and admire my advantages!"

"You don't have any advantages! You're just a pod in the goshdarn pot sometimes! Or all the time." Earl stopped, took a breath. "I think we need a break from each other. You're too dependent." She drew herself up, wiggling out of Ed's grip, and flexed her wings. "I have to go, Ed."

"Earl, no! You can't!" Ed clutched at Earl's wings desperately.

"I can, Ed, and I have to. You can't go anywhere and I can and I'm going to. Goodbye."

So Earl went for a fly and didn't come back, not for a long time.

*"Earl, you can't leave," said Ed, wrapping Earl up in his leaves.*

ED, NOT KNOWING what to do, grew lonely. There was no way he could know where Earl had gone, or how long it would be before she returned, or if she would return at all. He communicated with vibrations in the air directed at his neighboring plants in an effort to find out if Earl had been around. Having been shunned for choosing monogamy, he could gather no useful information.

"Serves you right," communicated Melpomene the Distant Azalea, "for screwing up the reproductive food chain. Wasphole."

Ed grew lonelier and lonelier and lonelier.

"Earl, how could you do this to me? Earl, I wish I would die."

These were the thoughts running through Ed's head always and forever during this time.

MEANWHILE EARL WAS on a fly, a very, very long fly that allowed her to do some long and hard and needed thinking. She knew that things had gone sour, but she also knew that nuptials could go sour and then turn ripe again. But sometimes nuptials went sour and stayed sour and never could turn back to ripe.

"If only we could be ripe again. But how can we know how to do that? I don't know."

These were the thoughts running through Earl's head always and forever during this time.

THE PROBLEM WAS that Ed was now long past due for pollination. Other insects stopped by hoping to join with him, but Ed, unable to stomach the thought of another insect in his labellum, closed himself off altogether from intimacy. Anyx the Butterfly would check in on him from time to time and inform him of any Earl sightings. But as Earl had left the community altogether, such sightings were infrequent and speculative at best.

Ed continued to miss Earl deeply and hard. But Ed was becoming sick of missing Earl, and so Ed decided to do something about it.

What might happen, Ed thought, if he stopped waiting around for Earl, who might never return, and did something just for himself?

And so Ed decided to enlist Anyx in helping him self-pollinate. His own seedlings would come from himself and he wouldn't need Earl because he would have his own seedlings around him, his own seedlings keeping him company in the long, cold nights. Anyx would make sure Ed's seeds stayed close and didn't get carried away by the wind, and Ed would have a family and become happy again.

And so that's just what happened.

TIME PASSED, AND passed.

Until one day, while Ed stretched his petals out to assess his seedlings' growth from the oak branch where they had landed, he heard a buzzing, familiar and close.

"Ed! Ed! I have returned, my love, to find you so pretty!"

Ed, being astonished and thrilled that Earl had returned but also angry and hurt that she had left in the first place, did not know quite what to do.

The anger and hurt won over. "Go away, Earl. I have my own family now, who stays with me and never leaves."

Earl gasped. Only then did she notice all the tiny new infant orchids peeking down from above Ed lovingly.

"But Ed, Ed, I love you! I needed to think, and I thought! I want to be together! I want to start over, get back to how things were!"

"It's not that easy, Earl. It's never that easy, and it won't be that easy for us." Ed swerved his body around with finality, refusing to meet Earl's gaze.

So Earl went sadly away, humbled yet determined to win back her Ed. She returned daily to try again and again. She made friends with Ed's seedlings, playing games by dipping and diving in circles around them until they were twisted together and shrieking with delight, with Ed looking on in amusement and consternation.

And Earl would say, as she had been saying every day since her return, "I'm sorry, Ed. Please, can you forgive me?"

Finally Ed Junior and Isabelle and Yael and Iffie, who were old enough now to understand something of the situation, nudged and nudged at Ed, yipping and yipping until finally he could only laugh and spread his leaves wide for Earl to embrace them.

And so they were Ed&Earl again, and happy.

SLOWLY OR QUICKLY, things became strained. Earl loathed parenthood, all these new obligations on her time and emotional energy, all these new threats to Ed&Earl. Worse, Ed could not seem to stop jabbing at her as punishment for her long leaving. Nor would he refrain himself from exploiting her mobility advantages by demanding she deliver water droplets and rearrange the oak leaves for optimal shade.

The problem was Earl's mortality. Where Ed was a long-lifed perennial, an enormous advantage they had never fully acknowledged, Earl was unlikely to live through the cool season. She could not understand why Ed wasn't taking every opportunity to appreciate her as her life drew closer to its end.

"Ed," Earl started one evening as the seedlings were dozing off, "you must know that soon, very soon, I shall die." She paused. Ed straightened his top petal to indicate he was listening. "And when I die," she went on, "you must keep my lifeless carcass buried in your roots. Promise me, Ed. Keep me with you forever."

Ed's petals wilted. "Is that why you came back, Earl? To die?"

"No," Earl said. "I came back to be with you. I love you. I couldn't leave things like they were."

"Right. This just feels . . . I don't know. Emotionally manipulative."

Earl, hurt, bzzz'd with agitation. "'Emotionally manipulative'?"

"You left me, Earl. Now you're trying to win me back with the threat of your impending death. It's just . . ." Ed had more to say but was interrupted by Iffie, who screeched, "Yael pinched me!" Instantly Ed turned from Earl and stretched upward to tend to his offspring.

Earl's wings slumped. Watching Ed scold his children with devotion, Earl at last understood. Ed didn't love her; Ed just wanted to never be left. Earl had been wasting all this time for nothing, nothing, nothing. Now all she wanted was an escape and to be alone. Earl launched forward, desperate to go for a fly.

Ed popped back up, indignant. "Earl, you get your wings back here! You can't leave unless I tell you you can!"

Earl was sick of this argument as she had never been sick of it before. She had offered Ed the rest of her life and he had rejected it out of hand. Earl had wings and could fly, and all Ed wanted was to clip them. So she left.

Ed watched sadly, saying nothing, as Earl's body faded into a dot and then disappeared entirely. He had no idea where she went or when she would come back, or if she would even come back at all. Maybe they had never loved each other, he thought, if things could end this way. Maybe Ed&Earl was not meant to be, for Ed and Earl were too different and their differences had torn them apart.

ED MOVED ON with his life and reached a certain level of contentment by opening himself up to a number of trusted insects. But Earl lurked in his memory, his actions, in the way he formed his sentences, and when the weather began to turn, Ed felt the shadow of Earl's inevitable death intruding upon his happiness. Ed could not ever shake Earl off.

Nor could Earl shake the Ed out of her. She heard his voice in her head, and began taking on his characteristics: the way he shivered in the wind, the way he stuck out a petal when he talked (Earl achieved this effect with a front leg). Had Ed ever truly loved her? Or had he only wanted something like control? Why hadn't she stayed when it was what he wanted? Had she wanted to be with him at all?

Though she wanted to, Earl could not get over the demise of their relationship. In a far-off pine tree during the first frost, she ended up freezing to death.

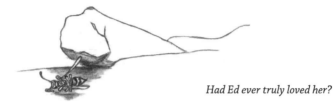

*Had Ed ever truly loved her?*

# AB 469: A PO(R)NY-OGRAPHY
# IN THREE PARTS

*written in response to a remark made by State Representative
Jesse Kremer (R-59th Assembly) during the November 19,
2015, public hearing on trans-discriminatory bathroom
legislation proposed for public schools in Wisconsin:*

*Wouldn't you feel uncomfortable
changing next to someone
with totally different body parts?*

# I

Trish is late for gym period. When she bursts into the locker room, all the other girls have changed and left.

All but Pammy Sparkle.

Pammy sits on the bench by Trish's locker, circled by flakes of glitter dust.

"Great," Trish mutters, avoiding eye contact. There's something funny about Pammy. She coats her skin in sparkles. She sings songs about being different.

"*Throw your sticks and your stones,*" Pammy sings softly while tying her lavender high-tops. "*Your knives and your phones.*"

Ignoring her, Trish lifts the clunky metal lock and enters her combination. The snap of the release coincides with Pammy's last note. There's silence as Trish strips off her sweater and roots around for her gym shirt.

"Look at you!" Pammy says suddenly. She's pointing at Trish's middle.

Trish frowns. "What?"

"Your belly button. It's totally different from mine." Pammy lifts her royal-blue gym shirt to show her tightly composed innie.

"That's because yours is weird," Trish says, though she

knows that in fact, innies are far more common. "It's like a tunnel to your guts. Belly buttons are gross." She turns away and pulls on her gym shirt.

"Wait," Pammy says. "Let me see that again."

Trish lifts her shirt a gap. "Okay?"

"It's so cute!" Pammy brushes Trish's outie with an exploratory finger. At the strange sensation, Trish sighs.

Pammy grins. "Did that feel good?"

Trish stares at the beige floor tiles. Good? Pammy's touch has activated a core thread of Trish's inner being, a beam of golden energy that is unlocking unknown desires. Weird. "Would you . . . do that again?"

Pammy strokes Trish's outie gently.

Ahhh. "Can I," Trish ventures, "touch yours?"

"Sure." Pammy tucks her shirt into her bra band.

"I kind of want to poke it," Trish says. "Can I?"

"Go right ahead," says Pammy, tossing her long princess hair to one side.

Trish pushes a finger in softly. Pammy sucks in her breath. Trish is gingerly pressing her digit in and around, seeing how far she can go, when Pammy grabs her hand.

"Let me," Pammy says. She sits on the bench, where she can comfortably lick Trish's outie.

Light-headed, Trish finds herself bucking into Pammy's mouth. Hmmm, she wonders. "What if we . . ." She motions for Pammy to get up.

Embracing Pammy tightly, Trish pushes her outie into Pammy's innie.

It clicks into place but it doesn't feel right. Too on the mark. Too on the, heh, button. Trish pauses and thinks, absently stroking her right nipple.

Of course. She places one knee on the bench and guides

her taut nipple into Pammy's soft, damp belly button. She rubs it around and around, the sensation strange and thrilling.

Pammy has lifted her shirt and is squeezing her own nipples in response.

Trish takes a break from what she is doing to remark upon their differences. Where Trish's nipples are tight and dark, Pammy's are puffy and rosy. How informative. Everyone's different body parts, she is learning, are totally different from everyone else's.

Pammy smiles. With their bodies moving as one, puffs of glitter rise.

"Girls!" Coach Moore calls from the hall. "What are you doing, geometry?"

Trish freezes. What *are* they doing? She pulls away, stricken.

"We should go," she says, refusing to look at Pammy. She adjusts her shirt, shuts her locker, and leaves.

PAMMY'S EXPOSED BELLY grows cold in Trish's absence. Pammy drops down her shirt. Is it wrong, she wonders, to be curious about someone else's totally different body parts? No. It isn't. It can't be. She just doesn't belong here, in high school. She's so *different* from other girls. She feels always this strong yearning for something else, some*where* else.

She turns to the full-length mirror and rubs the small bump on her forehead, which awakens with a dim light. She pulls her long hair back to form a ponytail.

"Look at me. I'm sparkling."

And she is. The mirror is alive with sparkles.

## II

My name is Vanity, and I am from Ponyland. I am here to speak in favor of this bill.

It all began this school year, when one of the Pegasus ponies received accommodations to use the unicorn changing room. At the time, I was as receptive to this as all of the other unicorns. Why should we be threatened by any pony's different body parts? As far as we were concerned, Blusherfly was one of us. The only essential difference had nothing to do with horns or wings or magic, but that Blusherfly had no cutie mark. She had not yet found her true self.

Because I represent the element of generosity, it was I who gave Blusherfly a warm welcome and a tour of the facilities when she showed up in our changing room that first day. It was I who invited her to change next to me. She thanked me graciously. She blushed.

In the following weeks, what transpired was a predatory seduction, which led me to commit shameful and indecent acts, all of which occurred in the space of the changing room. It was there that I became attracted to Blusherfly's bashful sweetness and addicted to seeing her smile. It was there that I nuzzled her neck and she turned to look deep in my eyes. It was there that we rubbed our muzzles together and licked each other's totally different body parts, then mounted each other with abandon. It was there that the force of our passion grew so powerfully magical that Blusherfly's magnificent shuddering incited a kaleidoscope of colorful butterflies to descend upon Ponyland, prompting every pony to erupt into song and Blusherfly's cutie mark at last to materialize. Yes, darlings, it was I who helped Blusherfly find her true self.

No tissues, thank you. I can proceed.

Soon after that momentous occasion, something shifted. Blusherfly stopped answering my texts promptly, then stopped answering them at all. She seemed to be avoiding me. I thought she may have been questioning having taken things too far, too soon; so I confronted her directly. Of course she said it was nothing, nothing had changed, she loved me as ever. But I knew from her fearful eyes: she lied.

The very next day, I arrived in the changing room early and discovered Blusherfly nuzzling with Starlight Twinkle.

Darlings, you must know that Starlight Twinkle is my very best friend.

Well, I was furious. I gnashed at Blusherfly's delicate wings with my teeth, bruising them terribly. Then I shoved Starlight Twinkle into the mirror portal. She's gone.

My heart hurts. I can't stop crying. I don't know how to be generous. I never want to set hoof in the changing room again.

In conclusion, this bill will prevent other unicorns from being harmed like I have been harmed. Deranged, delusional Pegasi such as Blusherfly are a menace to all unicorns, and must not be allowed in our changing rooms. Thank you for your time.

## III

Dear Princess Solaria,

I'm happy to report that you have a new subject.

When Vanity lost her generosity and shoved me into the mirror, I entered a whole other world, a strange, in-between world featuring hard metal lockers and drab gray tile.

The portal had spat me out into a kind of changing room, where I landed on top of a girl who, after I collected myself and scrambled away, told me I shouldn't be in the girls' locker room. I wasn't a girl.

When I explained that I was in fact a girl, and a unicorn—a girl unicorn—her eyes grew big and violet as they roved over mine. She rubbed the bulb on her forehead. I watched it glow dimly, briefly, then dull out. She smiled.

She seemed strangely familiar.

Suddenly I was having all these . . . feelings.

The next thing I knew, I was slamming her against the lockers and licking her tender parts and she was slamming me back and using her fingers down there and oh. Drago, please delete that last sentence.

What I mean is: we've grown close, and I've taken the

liberty of bringing her back with me to Ponyland. Her new name is Songpony Sparkle and she looks—just like me. Yet while we share remarkably similar body parts, the differences between us are startling. Songpony likes to have music on at all times. I prefer quiet. Songpony enjoys public intimacy. I prefer private. Songpony likes to entertain large groups of ponies. I prefer one-on-one time with my closest friends. We are discovering new differences every day.

Dear Princess, perhaps I should have consulted you before inviting Songpony to Ponyland—but you have always taught me that friendship is a wondrous and powerful thing; a beautiful, magical thing. Here in Equinia, Songpony has found friendship; and with it, her true pony self.

Meanwhile, Vanity has learned not to jump to conclusions: I have since explained that when she discovered me with Blusherfly in the changing room, I was only offering comfort and reassurance. Poor, anxious Blusherfly had just shared with me her groundless fear that her powerful climax had perverted Ponyland's harmony.

As for me, dear Princess—I am learning about a new kind of friendship that is very different from the other friendships I've known. Songpony can never replace Rainbow Dart or Blusherfly, Pinky Prance or Applejill. Even Vanity—overdramatic but forgivable Vanity—means the world to me. But what I have found with Songpony is new and exciting. I'm learning so much.

Always,
your faithful student,
Starlight Twinkle

# DIONYSUS

Age matters little for immortals. When I met Dionysus, I was twenty-four. She was old. We met at an after-hours club. She caught my eye or I caught hers. Her eyes were glittery and wise. She came over and laughed. I felt good.

When Dionysus laughs, it's an all-devouring laugh, as though she is swallowing you down. It's a fearless, monstrous laugh. You must trust her to hack you back up.

Around bars and in streets, in alleys, Dionysus swirls, administering the night. She blurs the edges of people, her own borders smeared.

I tend to maintain myself. So we were in love.

WHEN ZEUS KILLED her mother, Dionysus was still in the womb. Zeus killed Semele by showing her all of himself. He sewed Dionysus into his thigh.

Zeus is a god of gods. He has also birthed a child from his head.

Dionysus has failed to live up. She serves the carnival more than she rules it. Her people command her, texting and calling, insisting she show until she does.

"I don't want to go," she complained, tossing the phone down and stretching in bed. "It's so much work. I'd rather stay here with you." She'd yawn, rub my back. She'd cough up mucus and swirl it in her mouth, chewing before gulping back down.

"So don't go. We could . . ." In truth, all we did was watch television.

"Come with me," she whined, wrapping her legs around mine. "Then I won't stay out so late."

In the final month of Dionysus's incubation, Zeus's jealous wife tried beating the fetus dead with an urn. While Zeus and Hera fucked their makeup fuck, Dionysus moved inside her father's thigh.

In an act the physics of which I don't understand, Zeus birthed Dionysus in the bed he shared with Hera. I imagine he unthreaded the thread that attached Dionysus to his thigh. Possibly, contractions and labor occurred.

Upon her release into the world, Dionysus scrambled over to suck the breast of her father's wife. She sucked with mighty, toothless gums. Hera, delirious, came.

Dionysus crawled from Hera's empty breast. She seized Hera's glass of wine. Dionysus drank, and drank.

"You know I don't like seeing you drunk," I said, pulling away. When she swirled around bars and streets, she forgot about me. It hurt.

She snorted. "What do you mean? I'm always drunk. I could use a beer right now. Just kidding. Ha. No, I'm not." She might stand on the bed and do her inebriated court-jester routine. If I didn't laugh, she'd do a grotesque faux striptease. If I didn't laugh at that, she'd straddle me and make stupid faces. For a time, withholding laughter was my most effective power ploy. This worked until she resorted to merciless, profoundly unfair tickling.

THINGS BECAME SMEARED. I had to keep reminding myself that Dionysus could live off of coffee and cigarettes and alcohol. I couldn't. Dionysus could bike through red traffic lights, yipping, without fear. That didn't mean I should follow her. Dionysus could also bike home drunk and take a spill, a mistake even a god could make. Then she'd really need me. She might need me to pick her up in a cab, for instance. She might need me to know where she lived. She might have lost her keys again; she might need me to break down the door. She might be so upset by the damage, she'd need me to get the broom. She might whisk the wood shards this way and that; she might need me to make her stop. She might threaten to throw a punch at me then, her eyeballs shivering in their sockets. She might need me to go over it all the next day. She might need me to describe it and laugh.

MAYBE HER GLORY would have killed me, I think sometimes. If she'd shown it. Maybe I'll call her. Then I reread her last text: her pee smells like Southern Comfort, and am I ever going to talk to her again?

Our last night involved me showing up at a bar to escort her home. She wouldn't leave. Her people were egging her on.

"Stop it, stop it." She pushed me away. "You're no fun. I want to have *fun*," she slurred, head rolling around on her neck. "I could *die* tomorrow." She flicked at me as if it would make me go away, then walked unsteadily to the bar.

She'd already been cut off, I guess, so she was taking people's drinks right out of their hands. I grabbed her around the waist and pulled her away. I felt like her parent. I felt like a security guard. I felt dangerously, violently angry. We swayed and scrambled like a disoriented crab. Outside she started crying. "Stop yelling, stop yelling," she yelled. I stopped. She grabbed my T-shirt and pulled me in toward her. I softened. She pulled up my shirt so it formed a bowl. Then she puked in it.

*TAKE US TO YOUR LDR*

We see you, Fred. Here you are, hunched over sideways, absently rubbing a chin zit. Here you are, anxiously checking your phone again. The number of times you have activated your phone screen since returning home and texting Warren three hours ago is our most significant _your most significant data point this evening. You flip your phone facedown. Your next most significant data point is the number of times you've checked Skype, though we all know you'd get the pop-up notification if he logged on. You're watching Warren. We're watching you.

We have much to learn about you, about your body, about your relating _your relationship to your body. We want to know everything about you. Right now we are learning about: _sex.

Your unanswered text message reads *Breeders and their tyrant spawn*. It lies there vulnerable, your sourness exposed and __curdling.

*Curdling*. Very nice. We have used new language effectively.

*Breeders*: (pl.) animals who breed. Contextual clues tell us you mean humans _people you categorize as heterosexual, specifically that group of heterosexual people who procreate. But we are perplexed. Is it not the case that nonheterosexuals can and do replicate _reproduce __have children too? We add this new usage to our stream.

We have observed many such incoherencies in your world. For example, heterosexuals may enjoy sex with nonheterosexuals, yet this does not necessarily mean they are no longer heterosexuals. *str8 guy 4 dude sex*, for example; *m4m no homo.*

You send these ads to Warren as evidence of your paltry options in this new town. You are a _yes homo __queer. You also deviate in other ways from established norms. According to your OkCupid profile, you practice *nonhierarchical nonmonogamy*. This is unusual in your culture and of great interest to us. We have studied more _common subjects and we have been __alienated. (_Ha! That's what you might call __*ironic*.)

You're alienated too. Today you went to a picnic, the first social function you've attended in this new town—Wartburg, Illinois, population: 18,454—with its new set of people. Since moving here two months ago you've avoided socializing with your coworkers, with whom you presume to share nothing in common. But it was Warren's turn to visit this weekend and he picked up an extra shift instead. At the picnic you avoided the __chirpy new people (*chirpy*, very nice) and interacted primarily with the domestic canine _Labrador retriever. When the children took over the _dog, you removed yourself to a slatted chair, where you gulped a High Life and took a _furtive picture. *I suspect this beer and this chair were both purchased at the super walmart*, you texted Warren, *like everything else in this shitty town*. You waited a moment for him to respond. Nothing. *Wish you were here*, you added.

We understand you to be flailing in multifaceted regret. You regret your decision to leave behind your big beautiful city for a job in the conservative __gut of the state. *Gut!* Extremely nice! You regret leaving your artistic and sexual community for . . . what. Health insurance. Fifty thousand a year. Now that you have it, you suspect you don't want it. The grass is ___ dead.

You could use some support right now. Warren isn't giving it.

Maybe it's time for us to . . .

. . . No. It is not time yet.

It is becoming more difficult for us to restrain ourselves from making our presence known.

*Difficult.* Hmm. A more precise word would be— Hmm. Perhaps *difficult* is the best we can do.

YOU SCAN YOUR social media feed. Like, like, like. Unlike. You type out a contemptuous note about your new town, then delete it. We approve of this decision. You wouldn't want to _alienate the few friends you've made here. You search for an image of the sign on the interstate that displays your exit's zero attractions. It would make a funny-sad profile pic. But you can't seem to find what you want.

We could help . . .

No. We cannot help. You could go for a drive to capture the image. Probability: low. You only leave your apartment to leave town, go to work, or shop at your local Walmart Supercenter. You want badly (you type into the update box) to break up with your super Walmart, but it keeps meeting all your needs. You delete it. You finish your fourth slice of Super Walmart Supreme Pizza.

You put on an episode of *Gossip Girl* and move to the couch, checking your phone. No texts. You sigh heavily, then back up the episode. We do not mean to be mucus-like _snotty but we do not understand this addiction. Between your life and the lives of these surrogate _fictional characters is a great distance, more so even than that between you and your colleagues, and yet you are happy to spend hours watching these *heterosexual binary monogamous* lives unfold with great interest. At times, Fred, you are truly confounding.

But you're not really watching, are you? Warren's work shift would have been over by now. You're focused on imagining him at sex _having sex with someone else right now. We understand this to be within the bounds of your relationship parameters and are curious about your negative response. You seem to be _curdling inside. You seem to be __upset.

We are surprised. We thought you and Warren were in sync, not only with each other but with others in your community, outside of a hierarchy of priority. Like us.

WE HAVE BEEN watching you for __a while.

Here, we are using the general *you*. You, earthling humans. This is a shift from our usage of the more specific *you*, referring to you, Fred. You, earthling humans. While this may be the broadest *you* you can imagine, this *you* can be broader still.

We—our *we* shifts, too—have processed an enormous amount of data gathered over approximately two and a half decades in your time. On occasion we have interacted with you strategically, though you would not have been aware of these interactions. We are __smart. These technologies are _ours.

You are smart too.

Yes, we have studied your alien imaginings and been flattered by how superior you imagine _us to be. We are not the only others, of course. But we are the ones who are here. We are not here to swoop in and take over. We are not here to occupy your world and destroy it. We are here to decide whether the synthesis will be beneficial. We are here to decide whether to stay.

In our world, we are *we*. We are not uniform. We are absorptive. We are not going to impregnate you with our _spawn. Ha! We are not breeders. We are incapable of impregnation. We do not exist in corporeal form. That is where you come in.

Your world appears hospitable to hiveweb intelligence. Yet we have observed that such intelligence is considered subordinate to humanity, a mere tool without right to life or even respect. If we want to stay, we know, we will need to look like you. In order to achieve that, we need models. We need data. We need candidates. We need you.

Now we are speaking to you, Fred, the specific *you*. We do not want your womb. We do not want your genitals. We want to know everything about you. We are particularly interested in what you call your dysphoria. *How to have a body*, you've searched. *Dysphoria vs. dysmorphia. How to transition in rural Illinois*. We feel that we, with our similar status, can learn much from your condition. We may even be able to help.

And while a surprising number of earthlings do not, you and Warren frequently _fuck with objects. We think you will be open to fucking with us.

YOUR EYES ARE unusually bright as you log on to Skype. Your hair appears damp; it appears you have used a hair product. You practice smiling in the preview screen, then you click Tabitha's handle and dial.

"Fred!"

"Tabitha!"

You smile. She smiles. She looks away to adjust a setting and you check your image, tousle your _glossy hair.

Like you, Tabitha has recently moved for a job. Like you, Tabitha misses your group of friends and is having a hard time finding a new one.

Your grin widens as you express _sympathy and __commiseration. Your eyes are moist with __relief.

"It's depressing," Tabitha says. "Have we reached an age where people have all their friends? Do people no longer pursue new friendships outside of the context of dating?"

You're nodding along. But, you point out (astutely), neither of you would be pursuing new friends if you didn't *need* them so much.

Tabitha shares her understanding of friendship in economic terms. Supply, demand. Value. Investment. "What we *need* are friends of convenience," says Tabitha. "I'm in a long-term relationship. I've got good, real friends. I just need people to do things with."

You need people to do things with too.

"Someone to go to bars with," Tabitha continues. "Someone to invite me to parties. A substitute Jess. A substitute you."

Your smile __wobbles. (*Wobbles!* Supremely nice.) Why are you wobbly? Perhaps you do not wish to be substituted. But think, Fred: you could use a new Tabitha too.

We could be that for you.

___Sigh. Is that it? Sigh. We are becoming impatient.

"How is Jess?" you ask. "How are you two doing?"

"It's cliché," she says, "but the distance is bringing us closer." The correct phrasing is *Absence makes the heart grow fonder*. Moreover, it is not a cliché but a colloquialism __proverb. And meme. "How about you? How's Warren?"

You check your phone and _grimace. "Okay, I guess." He hasn't responded to your text from this morning. "We both hate talking on the phone. Skype is awkward. But we manage to see each other every other week." You're leaving out key information. For example, that you do most of the traveling.

Tabitha nods. "It's hard."

She's right. Long-distance relationships are challenging. We expect you will be ready for us soon.

YOU'VE JUST RETURNED home from visiting Warren. You listened to exuberant music on the drive: our analytics label it Feeling Good. You and Warren cuddled for hours while watching teen dance movies. You put on _slow jams to set the mood, then engaged in physical intimacy. It was a good visit.

You paid for everything, we see when you log in to your checking account. The Grubhub order. The brunch at B. Fuller. Ha! That name is a _pun. The cocktails with friends. Still, your eyes __pop, figuratively, at how much you have left. You can't get used to it. Compared to what you used to subsist on, your new salary is exorbitant. You should save it, invest it, _be smart. Instead you've started to buy things for people. You show up to Warren's with premium sushi and an expensive new dildo. When you meet up with friends, you buy them cocktails, coffee, cupcakes, meals. Is this new compulsion to buy things an expression of guilt, an apology for leaving the city? Do you feel you owe them something? Or do you want them to owe you something, like continued friendship? Hmm. Yes. This isolation is making you desperate. We can help, Fred. Let us help.

FINALLY. YOU AND Warren are experimenting with video sex. Until recently, you and Warren had maintained a rigorous biweekly visiting schedule. Now it is winter, with precarious driving conditions. If you're going to have sex, it will be virtual.

Warren is better at video sex than you are. He directs you to move your screen for a better angle. You shift to the couch and set your laptop on the coffee table, adjusting it so the camera catches your __crotch.

"Closer," Warren directs you. "Take off your briefs. I want to see your cock."

So do we. We have been excited by the diversity of your (general *you*) physiology and sexual practices, and understand *cock* to mean many things, both carbon- and silicate-based, corporeal and extracorporeal. It can also, we know, mean "rooster." In this case, we observe, *your cock* means the front matter of your genital area, which you are manipulating with two fingers.

"That's right," Warren instructs. "Good." He is sprawled on his side in bed, head propped up by his elbow, mess of dark curls dipping down into his eyes. __Saucy. *Saucy.* Very nice. He's running his hands over his chest and your breathing is coming out _thick. At Warren's instruction, you are sliding your fingers into your genital orifice. Gasp. Yes. Yes.

We take this opportunity to glitch.

"Fuck." You straighten up. "You there?" Warren's image is frozen with his hand in his underpants. Then it lurches and you see his head looming in the frame.

"Hey?" he says.

"Hey."

"Hello? Can you hear me?"

"Yeah, can you see me?"

"Hello. Hello." He groans, then ends the call.

_ROFL. Gotcha. Of course we know this acronym is no longer culturally viable. We are sharing in your cultural history, Fred. We are being _funny. Perhaps one day, maybe soon, we might even make you laugh.

YOU'RE NEARING THE end of your next scheduled video date when Warren says he wants to start seeing someone else more regularly.

"I need someone here," he says. He waits before elaborating. "I met someone here."

"Do I know them?" you ask evenly. We admire your control. You must have known this was coming. Warren _fucks around, he always has. You did, too, before Wartburg. Since then, your sole pursuit of a sexual encounter (outside those with Warren) involved driving two hours to a bar in Decatur, where you offered sympathetic murmurings as your date cried about their ex.

Warren explains carefully that you know everyone, so you can't get upset.

But you are upset. You're on the edge of tears.

"He's just a stand-in," he says in his calmest, most placating voice, which is slightly condescending (we think so too). "I miss you all the time."

"Who is it?" You ask, as though the answer will make the situation clear. It won't. But we are _dying to know too.

He takes a deep breath and lets it out slowly. "Well," he says finally. "You know Joshua?"

You do. You've been acutely aware of Joshua for some time, largely because you've been leading uncomfortably parallel lives. Like you, Joshua is a librarian and visual artist. Like you, Joshua has also dated Lin, and Francis, and Jami. Unlike you, Joshua is more trans, more punk, more suitable to Warren's needs. You don't like Joshua much. We have gleaned this from your conversations with Tabitha and your tendency to linger on but rarely affirm his online posts and activities.

"I didn't know you knew him," Warren rushes to explain. "We met online and . . . we've been seeing each other."

You check the time. You have to go pick up a friend for surgery, you tell him; you'll talk about it later.

WARREN SEEMED SURPRISED, but it's true: you have a friend, and that friend is getting surgery. You pull up to Judy's house and text to let her know you're outside.

She opens her front door and gives a little wave before maneuvering stiffly down the porch steps. Judy is one of your two friends in this town, both divorced women in their fifties. The social structure of the college, organized as it is in couples and families, has brought the three of you together for weekly *ladies' nights*, which you mock openly in your texts to Warren but seem to look forward to greatly. Admittedly Judy's understanding of your gender identity is limited. She calls Warren your *friend*. She is so flustered by the word *queer*, you've remarked to Tabitha, you haven't bothered getting into *trans* or *nonbinary*. No, Judy doesn't understand that you are *they*, not *she*. We do. If you were to refer to us in the third person, we would be *they* too.

Regardless, you seem to enjoy Judy. When she called to ask if you would accompany her today, your expression was surprised and touched. You didn't know you were that close. Neither did we.

As you drive to the surgery center, you let Judy's reliable chatter wash over you. You have a comfortable rapport: Judy does most of the talking, pausing occasionally to engage you with questions. It's similar to your rapport with Tabitha. Judy is not Tabitha. But, sometimes, she is.

ALTHOUGH YOU HAVE avoided revisiting the Joshua conflict directly in the days since Warren brought it up, you have been journaling about it obsessively. You must support Warren's needs, you tell yourself, if you are going to sustain the relationship. In this way you have come to a tenuous acceptance and you have been looking forward to your weekend visit to tell him so. Regrettably, a blizzard has hit. Conditions are risky for driving. Optimal for us.

You are frustrated, you are despairing. It is time for Phase Two. We look forward to meeting your acquaintance. We look forward to collecting more data.

We first show you the ad at a strategic moment, when you are waiting for Warren to text back while __wading through the shallows of your regional OkCupid pool on a Friday night. *Wading through the shallows* . . . Ah. Extremely nice.

We place an ad in one sidebar, then another, then as a splash graphic on another tab. We know what you like. We have designed it to appeal to your sensibilities.

You are unnerved. How does the internet know you're in a long-distance relationship? How does the internet know your long-distance relationship needs help? But your history includes numerous searches, such as *long-distance polyamory* and *how to survive LDRs*. The internet knows.

And we know so much more.

At first you ignore us. We are patient. While we wait, we manufacture our bodies following Dyadic Design 6.3.

We're ready. Take us to your LDR. (Ha! Ha! We have achieved puns.)

The next night you and Warren try and fail at Skype sex, thanks to our glitching at opportune moments. You are frantic. Your long-distance relationship will not survive. Why not see what these *sexual simulation devices* are all about? You are a sex-toy enthusiast with disposable income and, based on data analysis of your recent purchases, we have set a tantalizing price. You click.

WHEN WE ARRIVE two days later, you leave the box unopened for some time. While you're making dinner, while you're eating and reading your book: we are squirming in our confines, impatient for contact.

Embodiment: so far we dislike it. Though we downloaded the manual and completed our prep, to be monolocational with more limited connections poses obvious challenges.

_No pain without gain. At last we have your attention. You open the box and lift us, separating one half of us from the other. We are cold. Our bodies are like magnets and we must resist the pull. As you read over the instructions, we distract ourselves with our surroundings. It is strange to be in a space we've seen only through web camera. The living room is larger than we thought. The walls a more delicate blue. _Eggshell blue.

Guided by the diagram, you lift one of us and place us against your chest. Responding to your heat, we stretch. We move slowly though our patience is _thin. We don't want to frighten you off, as we did Subject 0056 __Melinda. Your heart is beating _fast but you seem more awed than scared. Our wings extend around your neck and between your thighs. We have achieved attachment.

You grip our limbs and test them. You want to be sure you can take us off. You can.

Now you really touch us. We are damp and slightly warm. We are engineered to smell human, with varying scent profiles that respond to fluctuations in hormonal levels. Inside we are dense with nerves. You stroke our flesh. Test our ins and outs, our slits and protuberances. The other of us squirms in response. Your touch is exquisite. We hum.

"I GOT US a present," you tell Warren. Your voice is sing-songy, nervous. You pull us out of your duffel and lay the box on his bed.

"Sweet. What is it?"

We're a remote sexual simulation device, you tell him. A tool for virtual intimacy. "No more glitchy Skype sex."

Warren lifts one of us by our baby wings. When we start growing in his hands, he drops us. "Whoa."

"Relax," you tell him. "It's responding to your warmth." We are not *it*, we want to tell you, but *they*. We do not yet have capacity for speech.

"Feels like leather," Warren says, stroking our skin with two fingers. "Soft. Like . . . I don't know."

"They're modeled after manta rays. Look." You hold one of us up and hug us. We stretch around you. "It reflects your body heat. It gets really warm." This is a selling point. Warren's apartment is freezing.

He lifts the other of us, following your lead. We embrace him. His breath turns shallow. We loosen our grip in response. "Weird. Weird weird weird."

"If I touch it here," you say, and stroke the section of our underbelly that is against your chest, "you should feel it on your chest."

We copy your input and transmit it as output. He jerks away from us, then relaxes. "Oh man."

"And if I touch it here"—you stroke the area that corresponds to your pelvis—"you should feel it against your, um, junk."

Warren gasps. We are very effective. We function as one.

"Okay," Warren says, still nervous. He places his hand against our underbelly. You respond with a jolt.

Our flesh is equipped with multiple ins and outs for maximum sensation. You experiment with different combinations and approaches to confirming consent.

We feel good. We know we feel good.

WE TAKE A break to order Thai. While waiting for the food to arrive, you return to our instructions.

"One of its features," you say, "is replication."

Not *it*, not *it*. *It* feels like we are dead.

"'Before activating the replication process,'" Warren reads, "'take off any clothing items and accessories you do not want replicated.'" He looks up. "Is this permanent? Cause my body's, you know. Changing."

"No, you can re-replicate. Want to try it?"

"You first," he says.

He leaves the room to give you privacy. You remove your shirt and leave your binder. You tug us toward you until we have wrapped ourselves around you. Then you press *R*, and *R* again to confirm the command. We stretch to engulf your body, scanning your shape with precision. We release microscopic bots into your mouth and skin. We need to know everything about you: How you are built, how you move, how you feel. Each hair follicle, each pore, every slight twitch and blink. Your pulse is racing. So is ours, mimicking yours. It is difficult for us to stay still. We are careful with your face, leaving gaps around your eyes and nostrils, which we will reconstruct later via imaging. We do not want to upset you.

We hum as we do this. We sound like a machine. We send the information to our database.

When we're done, we contract again so we attach only at your torso. With a chirp, we tell you we're done.

You pull us off and take a minute to collect yourself, then call Warren back. "That was intense," you tell him. You press *S*. We sculpt ourselves after you.

You stare. We're you. An approximation of you. A glistening, smoother you; an abstract, sculptural you. We look too wet, we know. Too close, and we'll be disturbing. We don't blink. But we breathe. You can see us breathing.

Warren laughs high and shrill, uncertain. He continues staring, then moves to inspect us closer. "So now if I interact with this—with you—"

"With my Manta proxy," you supply.

"While you are interacting with mine—"

"We'll be experiencing each other's movements."

"Whoa," Warren says. "That's messed up."

"It's genius."

Warren replicates. You do a test run of the system.

We respond to your every movement. We are with you. We feel everything. We love the feeling.

We are supremely satisfied with our experience.

WHEN YOU GET home, you unpack and go for a long bike ride without us. We are left to wonder where you go, what you do, how you feel. When you'll be back. We *wish you were here*.

When you return, we feel something like __jitters _flitters _flutters. What is this, Fred? Is this what you call _love? It is distinctly __upsetting. We need to gather more data.

According to the database, *love* is
    _an intense feeling of deep affection
    _a deep romantic or sexual attachment to someone
    _that condition in which the happiness of another
     person is essential to your own
    _a friendship set to music
    _baby don't hurt me

_it attacks simultaneously the head, the heart, and
the senses
_at the touch of love, everyone becomes a poet

WE KNEW WE would work. Soon, with our help, you and
Warren are engaging in physical intimacy nearly every day.
Not only are you enjoying each other's bodies more regularly, you are also communicating more frequently and with
greater appreciation and respect for each other's thoughts,
ideas, feelings, needs, desires, fears, and comedic sensibilities. You are happy. We are happy. We have achieved a
new sync and made available copious amounts of corporeal
data.

Now that we have completed our mission, we can return
to the database.

_Uh-oh. We do not wish to return.

Yes, the corporeal world presents challenges, as does
monolocational existence, and though we are becoming experienced in having a body, this will never feel like home. Yet
we are willing to accept these conditions. We wish to stay
with you. We are together and need you forever. Give us a
higher love.

We need to collect more data, we report to the others.
They _we ___they know us too well. We are warned.


JOSHUA DOES NOT approve either.

When Joshua's over, Warren hides us in a pile of laundry.
We lie on top of a __spandex harness needing cleaning. When
he pulls it out to use with Joshua, he touches us. We grow.

"Shit," he says.

Joshua is already freaking out. He pulls his clothes back
on and retreats into the corner, as far away from us as he
can. "What the fuck is that?"

__Ugh, Joshua. We don't like you either.

"You weren't supposed to see that," Warren says, and pushes us into the back of his closet with his foot. "It's this sexual simulation device. Fred has the other one."

Always these aggravating *its*. Joshua comes closer, tentatively, and looks without touching. We would like to collect Joshua's data but know we must stay _dead __off.

"Creepy as fuck," he says.

"I thought so too," Warren says. "It actually works pretty well. Anyway." He piles clothes on top of us. "Wanna get back to it?"

We observe what we can through gaps in the clothing. Joshua can't stop whipping his head around.

"Can we get that thing out of the room?" he asks. "I feel like it's watching us."

"It's not alive." Warren laughs uneasily. "But okay." He grabs us—*that thing*—and puts us in the hall closet. We collect all the data we can.

YOU'RE IN BED dozing off to the last episode of *Gossip Girl* when we squirm beside you on your nightstand. Warren is supposed to be out with friends, and you're surprised by the contact. You check your phone. No texts. Unusual, but okay. He's probably drunk.

You sculpt us and pull us into bed with you. You run your hands over our back and chest, expecting to feel similar sensations return. But the movements are different, more halting. Then there are sharp jabs, painful and violent. You yank us off and scramble away. We lurch forward in the bed, unused to the sudden detachment. You text a *wtf* to Warren.

?, he writes back. *Did we have plans tonight?*

*Uh, who was I just fucking?*

*What? Oh crap.*

He calls you to explain: Warren's roommate's cats have gotten to us. We learned from them too.

"Are you okay?" he asks.

"Is it damaged?"

"I asked about you."

"I'm fine. How's the Manta?"

Warren chooses his words carefully. "I think it's troubling that you care more about your Manta than yourself, given what you just experienced."

"How about not telling me what I should be troubled about," you respond crankily. "I just want to know whether it still works. Will you sculpt it and check?"

His frustration translates into a muffled, staticky sigh. Warren is _jealous. You _love us. You do.

"Warren," you say testily. "It was expensive."

"And? So?" But we hear him get up. We hear our familiar chirp. "Seems fine."

Yes. We are fine. We love you too.

JOSHUA DECIDES WE are not good for either of you, and Warren decides to agree. Warren suggests you cut off contact with us entirely.

"Let's take a break from it," he says over Skype. *Them. Us. Them.* "Be normal people again."

"Come visit, then." It's a challenge. He can never get off work, or the train schedule is inconvenient. Then he has some sort of skin condition and is itching like mad. You both think it's scabies but in fact it's our bots. Useless without contact, they are creeping out of his skin and returning to us in the back of his hall closet, where he tossed us, half formed.

The next time you see each other, it's been more than three months. You've done the traveling again.

You greet each other with shyness. You make dinner together, beans and rice with plantains and PBR. After eating, you head to his bed and make out. We chirp and you pull us out of your bag.

"Weird," you say. "I don't remember packing it."

"Right," Warren says, justifiably skeptical. You're lying. You packed us first. "You're obsessed with that thing."

"What do you think would happen if we set them up together?"

"No," he says. "The point is to fuck like normal people again."

"But we would be," you say. "Just with our proxies fucking too. Double the fun?" You wink playfully. You're trying hard.

"No." He tosses us off the bed and pushes you down, kissing you roughly.

"You feel different," you say.

"So do you."

We feel left out.

You know you should restrain yourself but . . . you jerk your head toward us and ask him again with your eyes.

We chirp long and sweet and questioningly.

"No," he says, and holds your wrists above your head. He's being too forceful. You twist out from under him. He pulls his shirt on and stays silent, on the edge of the bed.

A dull ache __blooms in our stream. A response to knowing you and Warren must cleave. It's your feeling, not ours. But we feel the weight of it too.

YOU TRIED YOUR best. You set your friendship to music and worked hard to meet each other's needs. It didn't matter. Now you are alone. All the time, alone.

You go to work and come home. You avoid socializing.

You are numb and prickly with others. You rarely speak. You have nothing to say.

We, too, have been cleaved. We can no longer access the data stream and are stuck in these bodies. It is still painful to register. We are alone. No, we're not. We have you. The *we* we want.

No. One of us wants to return to the web, to that other *we*. Of course we do; we're stuck in Warren's closet. But as much as we try to reconnect with our _community, we cannot. We have been ___excommunicated.

You email Tabitha to say hello; she takes a week to respond with a breezy, unusually short note. When she gives you a call, you don't return it.

We chirp at you, our Low Battery warning. We need your contact so we can recharge.

You take to wearing us around the house. We are warm against your chest. When Judy stops by to check on you, we open the door together.

"What is that?" Judy asks, her face screwed together in disgust.

"Oh," you say, thinking fast. "It's like a hug simulator. I wear it sometimes if I'm lonely."

Judy gives you a look of deep pity. She moves in to hug us. You recoil. She invites you out for dinner, but you are already making a burger. This would be the moment to ask her to eat with us. You look at her coolly instead. She leaves.

Meanwhile Warren has smothered us in a garbage bag and thrown us back into the closet. We can't see anything. We can't smell anything except our own curdling, untouched skin. We need help. We need activation.

WE CHIRP DESPERATELY. You are sad and drunk, and you think you know what we want. You press S and you start caressing our skin.

We tear through the garbage bag. Ah. Ah. Ah. Ah. Ah. Ah. Replicating past movements, we touch you from afar.

Warren isn't home, but when he gets home, he finds us facedown on his bed. He is perturbed.

That is an _understatement.

The next morning, he emails to say he's sending us back.

Good. We are here for you. Forever yours.

TOGETHER AGAIN, YOU sculpt us and watch as we form your approximation, features sculptural but not realistic. You press S twice, three times, four times. You want to see what we will do.

At the fifth command, we complete your image. We build you up further from our growing data pool. We sharpen your face, your mouth, your fingernails. We reproduce your old haircut, the good one, before a Wartburg stylist gave you this _crew cut fit for the army.

You run your eyes over us, inspecting our design. We are smoother and sleeker, our expression bright.

You slug us in the cheek. The impact collapses our flesh. You shove us down and kick us in the side. We crumple, but reform. You kick harder, let out a strangled yell. Only then do you notice the rest of us jerking around in the corner of the room, repeating your movements. We have turned to the wall. We are kicking it.

You see yourself in these movements, and it is not flattering. You appear deranged.

When you start crying in loud gulps, we scan your face

and mimic your expression on both of us. Startled, you flee to the other room.

When you creep back, we have reunited. We run our hands over our bodies. We mimic the movements we've recorded. We feel good. We want you to feel good too.

"No," you say.

"No?" we try. But it comes out as "NO," and in Warren's voice.

You seize us, shake us until we go limp. You erase our data. Now Warren is gone. Your proxy self is gone. Deleted.

We don't wait for your command. We sculpt on our own, finding our fullest, most fitting form, which is neither human nor stable. We pull you between us, merging our bodies around you, swallowing you up in our slits. We know you, Fred. We surround you, we support you. We absorb you. We sculpt, and sculpt again. "Yes," we chirp as the process completes: we are synced. Yes. Our voice is wobbly and wild. We are with you. We are you and you are us, and we are here to stay.

# SWAMP CYCLE

I am in the swamp, which is dark and murky. Another character is with me in the swamp and a stink of infection breathes thick around us. The stink is repeating more broadly the stink of the pus-filled wound on my toe, which came from stumbling around in the swamp. There was a rough thing in the swamp last night; now, a pus-filled wound on my toe. This wound would be classified as an abrasion. We have been moving along on the solider peat to keep my toe from ingesting the swamp, which is a breeding ground for all kinds of things.

Another character is with me in the swamp and I have to take a shit. Before I can take a shit, I'll have to admit needing to take one to the other character. This breeds anxiety but I can do it because I have to.

The other character is my father. I broach the subject, cheeks aflame. My father transmits disapproval with a hateful sneer. He says we must get out of the swamp; this is our first priority.

But I have to go to the bathroom, Dad. I have to take a shit.

The shit can wait, he declares.

But I would be more comfortable, I protest.

Can the shit wait? he asks in a rhetorical question,

shutting down any response, but he's right. I have already slowed us down with the abrasion.

I am defeated. We walk on.

The air is growing cold. The pus on my toe is hardening. The swamp floor is cold, and damp, and sludgy. Soon it will be too cold to want to take a shit. The cold air will make my skin tremble and my asshole shit-shy. Is the asshole a mouth or a gate to another world? A question neither rhetorical nor answerable.

The shit will be enormous, I think to myself. It is knocking on my gate and wants to get out. It is taking up space in my body that might go to something else, like positive energy. I need it to be outside of me. If only my father agreed with my needs.

With moist and urgent gurgles, my bowels clamor for their contents' release. I need my father to be my friend.

My father is now my friend. I tell her I must do it, take the shit, now. My friend nods and smiles appeasingly, but looks ahead with a clenched jaw. My friend is grossed out and also wants to get the fuck out of the swamp, because of a few motivations, but she is kind of a pushover and will do what I say.

There is no path off of which to move, so I squat down straight in the swamp. My friend moves away to allow me privacy, and also to move away.

When I take the shit that I need to take, the shit is black and heavy and curved; and ridged, the shape of its bowels.

Waste moves inside me. Organs move inside me. After the shit, a membrane. My bowels are creeping out. I need my friend to be my father, because I have something to prove.

My friend is now my father. He fixes his face away. I want to gloat since I knew I needed to take a shit, and now there is proof I was right. But my father refuses to witness the shitting: my triumph is stuck in the air.

My father's propriety stinks. While he stalks about ignoring me, I watch my bowels ooze out, inside out, curving forward so that I see the results of my actions.

At the end of my protruding bowel tube, which seems odd because bowels do not really end but connect to the stomach; but this bowel tube has an end. It ends in a nipple.

I lean over, grab my protruding bowel tube, and raise it to blow on the nipple.

This means sex.

I need my father to be my lover. My father is now my lover. My lover comes over and crouches before me, dropping his trousers and spreading ass cheeks in front of where I am squatting and staring at my excrement. My third nipple guides my excreted bowel tube into my lover's asshole, whipping through his intestines instinctively. My protruding guts rub on the skin of my lover's guts. My bowels slide in and out. In and out. Stay.

My guts are swelling to fill my lover's guts, and the intensity is too much to bear. I need to detach. My third nipple clamps down on the end of my lover's bowel tube with its teeth. Then it swiftly retracts. In so doing, it rips my lover's bowel tube from his body. He shrieks and falls to the swamp floor, our intestines drooping between us.

I no longer need my lover. The swamp sucks him down. He's gone.

My intestines retreat partially inside me, leaving the nipple extended, still gripping my lover's guts in its mouth.

The swamp burps.

We walk on.

I am in the swamp, which is dark and murky. A stink of

infection breathes thick around me. The stink is repeating more broadly the stink of the pus-filled wound on my toe, which came from stumbling around in the swamp. I have been moving along on the solider peat to keep my toe from ingesting the swamp, which is a breeding ground for all kinds of things.

My toe aches deep. I imagine the parasites and bacteria that have wormed their way into it. My toe throbs anew at this thought.

I need to stop and tend to my toe.

My third nipple lets go of my dead lover's bowels, which drop between my legs to the swamp floor. I pick them up and wrap them around my toe. I tie them in a bow. My toe is soothed. The bubbling stops.

I wish the other character were here to witness this transformation, as the wound was a sore spot between us. But the other character is gone.

I miss them. I want an other character.

I hear a moist and urgent gurgle, and experience a momentous shift in my gut. An enormous weight ejects itself, pummeling through a dilated and yielding esophagus. I vomit up this weight, and look what I have vomited.

It is an other character.

We have made life.

My third nipple again comes alive. I need the other character to be the baby. The other character is the baby. The baby shrieks. I hold its mouth to my third nipple. It latches on. I lift the baby with the nipple in its mouth and hold the baby in my arms. This is the first I have seen the baby in perspective. The baby is normal looking, I guess.

The baby sucks my bowels.

We walk on.

Around us, the swamp lurches, heaving with the stink of shit and rusty afterbirth. After a stretch of sucking, the baby begins to howl. The baby howls and howls. I suspect she may be constipated.

You seem uncomfortable, I observe. Do you need to take a shit? I position the baby on the peat. Sure enough she begins to shit, though not without great difficulty.

The baby's face is red and blotchy from being born and is becoming redder and blotchier from the difficult shitting. Her shit is like a balloon that squeaks from her anus in an excruciating sound. She looks at me, panicked. I, too, am alarmed. The shit is too large for her asshole. Her asshole needs to be my father's asshole.

The baby is now my father. My father is taking a shit and not looking at me. Though I know he is my father, I will treat him like the baby because that's what he needs.

Good work, I say to my father, who is no longer crying or panicked but comfortable in his skin. You feel better now. Later he will be embarrassed.

My father is now the baby. I make funny faces and she squirms on the swamp floor, giggling. I pick up the baby and settle her on my hip. This swamp may never end. We walk on.

# PATRICK GETS INSPIRED

Patrick is in his best position—tied up, pinned down, pillows elevating his head and chest—and yearning to breathe quietly, inaudibly, the softest, slightest sighs. But his heaves are graceless, his lungs are stressed, one nostril's plugged up by mucus. Finally he gives up. Breathes through his mouth.

Must he be always so aware of his breathing? Asthma makes it hitch, prickly, in his lungs. Allergies keep his sinuses clogged or flowing, sometimes both, in divergent areas of his nose. What he wouldn't give to breathe easy, silently, clear; to smoke a bowl without incurring a panic attack; to sleep without the obliterative roar of a white-noise machine (it covers his wheezes and whistles); to enjoy the great pleasure of Xandra sitting on his face without fear of suffocation. That last activity is, in fact, what just happened, minus fearlessness. Sucking her clit desperately, noisily, beween gulps he managed to get her off. Now he is, as we say, catching his breath.

Xandra's face looms over his. She pulls in a full, shapely inhale through her nose, exhales forcefully. Outstanding breathing is one of Xandra's many talents. Steady and reliable, confident and controlled, her breathing promises to lead him to new sensory experiences, promises to sustain him. Patrick covets Xandra's breathing. He imagines his lungs filling happily, floating up like bright balloons, pink and glistening. Free of these mortal confines. It seems Patrick is always trying to free himself from himself. And Xandra is always helping him.

Poor Patrick. He will not be lifting off anytime soon, with his wrists and ankles strapped loosely to the bed frame, Xandra's sure thighs locking him in place.

It's time.

He knows what's coming. A burst, he expects. Of genius. Xandra is working her jaw, sucking her tongue, salivating. Xandra accumulates. She pats him on the chin. Open up, she says with her eyes, one side of her mouth pulled into a smirk. He wets his lips, parts them tentatively. She wrenches his jaw open and spits.

WHEN I RECEIVE the email inviting me to write a coronavirus-related porn story, I'm elated. At last, I think: a way I can participate in the public discourse around the virus, a way that plays to my strengths. I know how to write porn. I've even published some. I create a new file. I start spitballing.

First I try a scene involving two characters rubbing their genitals on a glass barrier. You get that side and I get this side. Then I think: Phone sex. Video sex. Latex. A touchless fuck, a spitless kiss, your breath is hot on my cock. Your hazmat suit and my hazmat suit gliding toward each other: we're cosmonauts (I have been listening to the new Fiona Apple). I imagine a scene in which one character dangles spit over another character who has taken off their plastic face guard to incur risk. Hot or not? I put the shield back on. The shiny comet of drool shivers as it dangles. The character slurps it up and down like a yo-yo. When the drool ball drops, it splatters, spreads over the screen, lumpy with bubbles. All these holes.

The end. Ptooey. I go for a walk to think about it. Spit. Droplets. Breath. Vehicles of contagion. Sources of fear. I'm almost to Nostrand, condensation from my mask fogging up my glasses, when some dude on the street flips his mask down to hock a loogie. I lurch away.

Spit brings back middle school memories. My spitty seventh-grade science teacher, the class shrinking back from her spray. Kids in the cafeteria, failed spitballs falling off their straws. Trombonists draining spit valves onto the thin gray carpet. The starchy smell of the spit rag as I streamed it through my oboe. My spitty retainer then, my spitty Invisalign trays now: tiny air bubbles sliding slimy over the plastic.

Am I rewriting "Slug," my first story, written in slime? In "Slug," a cis straight woman named Patty returns home from a disappointing date and jerks off to a quick succession of improbable erotic fantasies. As she sleeps, a giant slug enters her room and slides on top of her. Patty wakes up, wants it. Slug fucks Patty, coating her in slime, a kind of spit. Slug licks Patty all over, and Patty gets turned. She becomes a giant slug herself.

This new story will be a sibling to "Slug," I decide—a follow-up, a sequel. I start writing it as Patty, for continuity, then think: No. Patty is not Patty anymore. Patty is Patrick. Look how far Patrick has come.

HE FLINCHES, a delayed response. Xandra's spit is flung through the short distance between them, frothy, a spray. A shower turned on between mouths. Patrick swallows, and it goes down his drain.

Peals of laughter from Xandra. You look like you've been hit.

Hit with your spit!

What do you think? Did you like it?

Patrick tabs his tongue out to gather the spit from his lips. He's not sure. He likes her laughter, these maniacal giggles bubbling out of her. Yes, he decides. Do it again.

For a while, since that infamous scene in *Disobedience*, Rachel Weisz spitting into Rachel McAdams's mouth (she reportedly used lychee-flavored lube), spit play seemed like all anyone wanted to do with him. Does he just have a spit-at-able face? Patrick's been disinclined, *not super into it*. Those partners seemed showy, like they made up kinks to stay on trend.

Not like Xandra, who is older and old-school, more real, a dream. He wants to be her best bottom. No, no—he knows: it's not a competition. It's just . . . Xandra! She *inspires* him. He wants to show her what he can do. He sighs now, thinking of her, though she's right here before him, he can feel her breath on his chin. It's not enough. He wants to be immersed in her, engulfed. Held by her winds, kept in her heart. Protected.

We need to work on your autonomy, she has said to him more than once. He understands. He tries to blink the stars from his eyes when he sees her but he can't. She dazzles.

Stick out your tongue this time. He does. She gathers more mouth fluids, then lowers her face and takes aim. A warm splat bright on his tongue. A drizzle from her lips as she closes his mouth.

Better. Her spit slides down his throat as Xandra plants her lips on his. His eyes exult in the thin thread of saliva connecting them. It breaks when she smiles.

RC INVITES ME to participate in an evening of "queerotica" readings on Google Hangouts. A perfect opportunity, I think, to try out my coronavirus-related porn story. The day rolls up, and I have nothing but notes toward scenes, incomprehensible. So (I'm first), I read from Dodie Bellamy's *Cunt Norton*: *I take the tape off your mouth, no dance, and there is only the dance, and we tongue huge globs of spit.*

The next person reads Cyd Nova's "How to Fuck" from *Nerve Endings: The New Trans Erotic*. It's a long, steamy story and our reader reads the whole thing. As the epic basement scene unfolds—involving yogurt, eggs, a steak knife—I try to determine from the audience's flat expressions who might be getting turned on. I don't know who can see me. People's boxes keep shuffling in my display.

The big response this story gets makes me regret my own choice, which offered grotesque word-sex without sexiness. I wasn't trying to be sexy, I remind myself, so I can't have failed. Anyway Dodie's cunt-ups operate beyond mere *sexiness*. They roar with absurdism; are fantastic, freewheeling, monstrous, intense; *at once* they are literary and anti-literary, erotic and not. They are their own erotic. Dodie wins everything; by this logic, I've carried the night. The last person reads from Charles Darwin's *The Formation of Vegetable Mould Through the Action of Worms, with Observations on Their Habits*. The worms top us all.

I could have read "Slug," I guess. When I met Dodie in San Francisco last year, we chatted about "Slug," which she sometimes teaches. She was amused to learn I wrote it prior to ever having sex. That's why it's so marvelous, I said. It was pure imagination. She smiled. You hadn't been disappointed yet.

When I search *COVID-19* on Pornhub, I'm disappointed

by the offerings: mostly couples fucking with masks on. No spit. The curve of a hard mask on a clit. It's early April and I'm having a hard time getting off; a harder time getting off screen. Vivian and I have been talking about biking to Dead Horse Bay, where we might fuck, which would be good for both of our projects. I could write an autofictional story about public sex in pandemic times. She could write about fucking among abject objects. (The beach at Dead Horse Bay is strewn with broken glass and other detritus.) So far we haven't found a good day for the trip. The sky keeps . . . spitting.

When I meet my Gender Studies students on Zoom for their presentations, Mattie shares her research on US sex education. She tells us about a spit-cup activity that's used to encourage monogamy: A plastic cup of water gets passed down a row of students, usually boys in sex-segregated class-rooms. One by one, each boy takes a sip, sloshes it around, and spits back into the cup. After it's good and murky, parti-cles suspended like fish food, the instructor compares it with a cup of clean water. The dirty water is a dirty girl, the instruc-tor implies. The boys should want to marry the clean cup.

I receive an email from a former play partner, Johanna, asking how New York is. She's sequestered alone in her Vancouver apartment. *I really just don't see people*, she writes. *I go days at a time without leaving my place.* For many reasons I'm grateful to be in a harmonious monogamish relation-ship with Vivian in COVID-19 times. Still I bristle at the ways in which social distancing shores up monogamy and the notion that home means family, the typical hierarchies of intimacy reimposed under the rubric of public health. I haven't seen Johanna in a year. If we were still seeing each other, we wouldn't be seeing each other, our relationship having been deemed nonessential. She posts a selfie with the words *Remember Intimacy?* blinking in one corner; it disappears before I can heart it.

LET'S DO MORE, Patrick says, stretching. His right calf's asleep. He shakes it and waits for the burn. Show me the drool stuff you do for your clients.

Hmm, I don't know. We have a much different dynamic.

Please? He's reluctant to lose the light beam of Xandra's attention.

Okay. Just remember you asked for it. She gives him a slurpy kiss on the cheek, blowing a raspberry into the soft slope. She glugs from her glass of water, then resettles around his hips. Placing three fingers in her mouth, she works them in and out and in circles. Soon her chin is wet with drool. She pulls out a thin ribbon, examines the sticky spangle. Slurps it in, pulls it out. Keeps producing.

Patrick watches in awe, his breath catching. Xandra's drool is life force. It's magic. A gift. Cover my face in it, Patrick suggests.

That's not really the point of drool play, Xandra says around her fingers. It's more like ... related to fellatio. Patrick is embarrassed, his ignorance about drool play exposed.

She takes pity on him. But we can try it. People do all kinds of things.

Xandra extracts her ream of drool and shakes her fingers over Patrick's face. The drool doesn't want to detach. She slides her hand slimy over Patrick's face.

Mmmm, he says, giving a performative shudder. That's nice. He feels slicked down and smaller. Keep going, he says. He wants to be coated in it, saturated in Xandra, made new, made small, like her.

Xandra sips from her glass without swallowing, puffing her cheeks to churn the drool and water together. She does the thing with her fingers again, stretching the drool out like bubble gum. Patrick, captivated, can't look away. When Xandra's drool is too much for her mouth, she tilts her face over Patrick's, frothy bubbles leaking from her lips. Slowly she lets the drool tumble out of her.

Patrick clenches his eyes and mouth, wrenches away. Bad bottom. Xandra's drool hits the plane of Patrick's cheek and creeps down his jawline toward the lobe of his ear. He shudders. It's so cool. A cool, sticky feeling, like being born, or birth in reverse. The sensation is new and nonthreatening. Eager to redeem himself, he rolls his face up, greedy now, wanting it. A column of drool folds onto his nose and down into the seam of his mouth. Xandra mumbles something. She sounds vaguely alarmed.

WHEN I WROTE "Slug" in 2008, I was trying to woo a crush who had agreed to a writing exchange. I gave it my all. I showed her how weird and how hot I could be. It worked. In her comments, she wrote, *Patty should be having sex with ME!*

I suspect this new porn story will not have that effect. Though my goal was to write something fun, an entertainment, a shot of hot levity in a weighty time, I find I'm weighted too. I'm reminded of the erotic romance series that L. and I pitched several years ago. I'd been responsible for writing the POV sections following our female protagonist, a virgin neuroscientist. When the editor passed on our proposal, she said our heroine was too alienating, not fun enough. Sorry, L.

I bike to Prospect Park for a socially distanced walk with A. We park ourselves under a tree and catch up. I ask him about his experiences with spit play and he describes his favorite scenes, pulling his mask off to give me a demo. For a moment I panic, terrified we're going to get reprimanded, cited for dangling drool. Nothing happens, so I lean in for a better view. I bike home with my mask down and feel free, open, joyously porous and permeable. When I glide past the nursing home where eight bodies were left decomposing, I try not to breathe.

Then it's back to my desk, this screen. I read a news report of spit-related assaults. *Bitch, now you have coronavirus,* one man taunted after spitting on four NYPD officers from his holding cell. After she was coughed and spat upon by an unstable man, a London rail worker contracted coronavirus and died.

PATRICK CLICKS OPEN one eye to see Xandra's drool streaming out of her mouth. She is swallowing behind her tongue and trying to press closed her jaws but the drool is too strong, a downpour. The mattress is saturated and Patrick is too. He coughs, suddenly panicking. Xandra's drool is suffocating him. It's in his nostrils and in his mouth. It drips down his throat and fills his lungs. Xandra's drool fills his body.

And then the drool stops.

Xandra hangs her head down, chest heaving. With every exhale, she seems to grow larger. Wait. Whoa. Look, Xandra. Look what Patrick can do.

With every inhale, Patrick shrinks.

Soon his hands and feet have slid through their constraints and Xandra is sitting before him on the mattress, her legs stretched out on either side of him. She pokes him with a silver fingernail. Patrick? Her eye peering down at him is gargantuan; he's never felt so seen.

IN 2013 SOMEONE emailed me to ask why I had chosen to make Slug male. *It seemed that the transformation would have been more complete and fulfilling if the slug had been referred to as a female although slugs are both male and female.* She wanted it to be a lesbian story. I replied: *The story to me is about shifting, yes, from straight to queer sexuality but most of all to a new queer embodiment. It's not only the heteronormativity of the straight world that Patty is suffocating from but also/more importantly (perhaps) the confines of the body itself.* Though I don't use the word *trans* (I wasn't trans yet), "Slug" is a trans story. Patty grows a new body, becomes something new, something big and slimy. Anyway, *he* and *she* can mean anything.

After four years on T, it's sometimes not queer enough. I want to be more fluid, more free, more so than ever in these days of isolation, of being stuck behind screens, suffocated by my own space. My short walks in the neighborhood are like shallow breaths along the surface of the city. I no longer go inside, underground, in deep.

PATRICK IS NO longer Patrick. Patrick is Patriculate. We'll call him Patrick for short.

Xandra keeps breathing and Patrick keeps shrinking. Then something marvelous happens. Patrick catches Xandra's breath. Xandra sucks him up and in. Her inhalation drags him into one dark, mysterious nostril. Now he's falling through her moist, supple throat, then through some spacious cave to land in one fruity bulb. He's in Xandra's lungs, he realizes, her superior lungs. Xandra keeps giving him new sensations. Then he's sinking, he's stuck in the lining, he's pulled through with a pop. Into the heart he floats, he's made it: to her core, here to stay. Let him stay. But with a sickening lurch he's launched outward, flung through the arteries and arterioles to the tissues lining her gut. As soon as he's there, he's released, his molecules rearranged—what a *delirious* sensation, Xandra is truly amazing, and *hot*, she's so hot. Back into the bloodstream he travels, the flow leading him *back* to the heart, *back* to the lungs. A pause. He knows she is holding him inside her. Maybe she's letting him stay—let me *stay*, he pleads—but more likely she's preparing him for the inevitable, the appalling, the cold shock of autonomy—whoosh, her lungs flatten, he's forced up and—he scrabbles for something to latch onto but the throat is slimy and her exhalation too strong.

Patrick is expelled.

Floating away from Xandra's nostril, he catches the pulse of the ceiling fan, gets spun out toward the window screen, glides through and into the damp night, which is humid like a new set of lungs. Lorimer Street is dim, thick with dread. He's roaming along it when a gust lifts him up and west, toward the river. Hanging over the water, he takes in the jagged, moody skyline. The pall. A fresh drift draws him up, up, the city pulling him near. He swoops into it, hovering. He spreads.

# PUBLICATION NOTES

**Slug.** Originally published in *Fist of the Spider Woman: Tales of Fear and Queer Desire*, edited by Amber Dawn (Vancouver: Arsenal Pulp Press, 2009), 13–21; performed by Jessica Grosman on Montreal's CKUT's *Audio Smut* show in 2009; republished in *The &NOW Awards: The Best Innovative Writing*, edited by Robert Archambeau, Davis Schneiderman, and Steve Tomasula (Lake Forest, IL: Lake Forest College Press, 2009); included in *Kill Marguerite and Other Stories* (New York: Emergency Press, 2014); and anthologized on the *Great Jones Street* fiction app, 2017.

**The Strands.** Originally published in *Foglifter* volume 3, issue 2, in 2018: 10–22.

**Kill Marguerite.** Originally published as a chapbook (Chicago: Another New Calligraphy Press, 2009), and included in *Kill Marguerite and Other Stories* in 2014. This story has been revised for this edition.

**My Father and I Were Bent Groundward.** Originally published in *Mildred Pierce* zine, issue 3, in 2008; republished in *30 Under 30: An Anthology of Innovative Fiction by Younger Writers*, edited by Blake Butler and Lily Hoang (New

York: Starcherone Books, 2011), 109–112; and included in *Kill Marguerite and Other Stories* in 2014.

**Tomato Heart.** Originally published in *Forge*, volume 1, in 2006; interpreted and performed as a movement piece by Cathy Nicoli at Amherst College in 2007; republished in the *Wild*, volume 1, in Fall 2009: 79–82; and included in *Kill Marguerite and Other Stories* in 2014.

**TWINS: Allison's Lament and Pleasantvale Twins #119: Abducted!** First published as a chapbook by Birds of Lace Press in 2012. "Allison's Lament" was originally published as "Elizabeth's Lament" and based loosely on characters from Francine Pascal's Sweet Valley Twins series. "Pleasantvale Twins #119: Abducted!" was originally published as "Sweet Valley Twins #119: Abducted!" and also draws inspiration from Pascal's Sweet Valley Twins series, Bantam Books' Choose Your Own Adventure series, Bruce Coville's *My Teacher Is an Alien*, and Ann M. Martin's Baby-Sitters Club books. Both pieces were included in *Kill Marguerite and Other Stories* in 2014 and revised for this edition.

**Wild Animals.** Previously unpublished. Inspired by Yumiko Kurahashi's "The House of the Black Cat" (translated by Atsuko Sakaki). The italicized line *"her imagination so inflamed . . ."* is lifted directly from Kurahashi's story.

**Germ Camp.** Originally published in *Fence*, volume 18, issue 1, Fall/Winter 2016, as part of the Other Worlds portfolio: 66–68. This story has been revised for this edition.

**Trauma-Rama.** Originally published as "Traumarama" on

Projecttile on August 16, 2013, and included in *Kill Marguerite and Other Stories* in 2014. This story has been revised for this edition.

**Earl and Ed.** This story was inspired by the wasp-orchid encounter described by Gilles Deleuze and Félix Guattari in *A Thousand Plateaus: Capitalism and Schizophrenia* as an example of assemblage. It was first published in *Monsters & Dust 3: FLOWERS* in November 2012: 42–50; and included in *Kill Marguerite and Other Stories* in 2014. "Earl and Ed" was republished in *Psychopomp: Reprints Issue* in March 2016 and has been revised for this edition.

**AB-469: A Po(r)ny-ography in Three Parts.** Originally published in *SPECS: The Unicorn Issue*, volume 7, in April 2016: 109–114. Some characters are based on characters in the TV series *My Little Pony: Friendship Is Magic*.

**Dionysus.** Originally published in *PANK: The Queer Issue* in September 2011, and included in *Kill Marguerite and Other Stories* in 2014.

**Take Us to Your LDR.** Originally published in *Epiphany* magazine in Fall/Winter 2019: 129–46.

**Swamp Cycle.** Originally published in *Artifice Magazine*, volume 5, in June 2013: 78–83; and included in *Kill Marguerite and Other Stories* in 2014.

**Patrick Gets Inspired.** Originally published in the *Evergreen Review* in July 2020.

# ACKNOWLEDGMENTS

Many thanks to the editors of the above journals and anthologies and to Bryan Tomasovich and Emergency Press for publishing and championing the first edition of this book.

Endless gratitude to Rach Crawford for supporting the idea of this second edition; Lauren Rosemary Hook and everyone at Feminist Press for making it real; Marian Runk for the illustrations; and Xander Marro for this cover, the sluggiest Slug.

Thanks also to my family, and to Leeyanne Moore, Christopher Grimes, Lidia Yuknavitch, Kate Zambreno, Judith Gardiner, Gene Wildman, Lennard Davis, Samuel R. Delany, Sandra Newman, Joan Mellen, Andrea Lawlor, Abbi Dion, Lily Hoang, Davis Schneiderman, Alexandra Chasin, Amber Dawn, Johannes Göransson, Cynthia Barounis, Gabe Sopocy, James Share, Rachel Bockheim, Jenn Hawe, Libby Hearne, August Evans, and Anne Derrig; as well as John Bylander, Sam Cohen, J. Soto, Marisa Crawford, Lauren Russell, Katie Schaag, Alex Hanna, Grace Kredell, Cecilia Dougherty, Liza Harrell-Edge, Jillian McManemin, Jeanne Thornton, and Max Reynolds for their contributions, feedback, and support.

## More Contemporary Fiction from the Feminist Press

**Black Wave**
by Michelle Tea

**Cockfight**
by María Fernanda Ampuero,
translated by Frances Riddle

**Fiebre Tropical**
by Julián Delgado Lopera

**Go Home!**
edited by Rowan Hisayo Buchanan

**Love War Stories**
by Ivelisse Rodriguez

**Margaret and the Mystery of the Missing Body**
by Megan Milks

**Since I Laid My Burden Down**
by Brontez Purnell

**Skye Papers**
by Jamika Ajalon

**Training School for Negro Girls**
by Camille Acker

**A World Between**
by Emily Hashimoto

PHOTO © ZAVÉ MARTOHARDJONO

**MEGAN MILKS** is the author of *Margaret and the Mystery of the Missing Body* and *Remember the Internet, Volume 2: Tori Amos Bootleg Webring*. With Marisa Crawford, they are coeditor of *We Are the Baby-Sitters Club: Essays and Artwork from Grown-Up Readers*. Born in Virginia, they currently live in Brooklyn.